THE
Swan Song
PENTAD

THE
Swan Song
PENTAD

BY
STANLEY L. ALPERT

ALPERT'S BOOKERY, INC.

This is a work of fiction. Names, characters, places, and incidents either are a product of the author's imagination or are used fictitiously, and any resemblance to actual persons, living or dead; events or locales is entirely coincidental.

Published by
Alpert's Bookery, Inc.
POB 215
Nanuet, NY 10954

Library of Congress Catalog Card Number: 98-93484

ISBN 1-892666-02-2

This book is printed on acid-free paper. ∞

Manufactured in the United States of America
September 1998

In loving memory of Rose Alpert

ACKNOWLEDGMENTS

I want to extend appreciation to all those who have helped hone and complete this book; their assistance and support were truly valued.

Kudos to Beverly Bierman for her continued help and extremely valuable input and contributions.

A special thanks to Linda Bland. Her friendship, editorial professionalism, and literary expertise are to be highly respected and admired.

And to Susan and Sharon for their everlasting devotion.

the golden swan

THE
SWAN SONG
PENTAD

City Life

ONE

An elderly woman trudged along the sidewalk. Though the weather was warm, a winter coat hung loosely from her shoulders. Her filthy, unkempt hair blew unbridled in the breeze, with only a faded, misshapen hat taming it at all. In one hand Alice Trumbel carried a large black pocketbook and a shopping bag; with the other hand, she dragged a shopping cart. Occasionally, she would stop to rest and survey her surroundings.

Sweat poured from her face, but did not seem to bother her. Stopping by a trash receptacle, Alice skillfully reached inside and felt around among the contents. Withdrawing a deposit bottle, she placed it into her shopping bag and moved ahead. Over the years, her specific route rarely deviated. By midday, she had reached the small park and looked forward to a brief rest. Approaching a wooden bench along the commons' perimeter, Alice plunked down. She consumed a piece of stale bread from her shopping cart. Its unpalatable taste remained long after the food was eaten. Securing the cart to her arm with a short length of rope, she watched as children played nearby.

A faint smile wrinkled her contours as one child tagged another and ran. *Tag* she thought to herself. *How long ago it was.* Following the children as they frolicked, her eyes twinkled as she reminisced. Clutching her pocketbook she permitted her fatigued body the infrequent luxury of a short period of relaxation.

A loud sound snapped Alice back to reality. Once again it struck, this time sending reverberations through the wood on which she sat. "Come on lady, get moving." She looked upward and saw a uniformed policeman who had struck the bench with his club. He repeated his command. "Come on, lady, you can't sit here."

"Why not? It is still a free country, isn't it?" she softly replied.

"Not for now. The mayor does not want any loitering in the park. Just do me a favor and move on."

"I don't understand. I didn't break any laws."

"Look, I only enforce the rules and until this parade and celebration are over, I'm afraid you can't sit along the route."

"What parade?"

"I don't have time to explain. Just get moving." She gathered her possessions. After scrutinizing the young officer one last time, she left the park and wandered up an adjacent street.

4

T W O

Journalists from every news service and publication were preparing stories on the city's metamorphosis. The ten-year plan would be completed in a month and the results were even more startling than expected. The archaic had been replaced by the modernistic as colossal glass and steel skyscrapers filled the downtown. Most of the remaining brownstones had been refurbished; they contrasted magnificently with the towering, glossy edifices.

What had once been a bold, idealistic plan was becoming a reality for all the contributors; huge corporations and businesses had been attracted by the city's revised tax package and other special growth incentives. New retail shops were packed with merchandise in anticipation of the celebration. Mayor Thompson's edicts reverberated through the city's work force; the streets were frequently cleaned of debris while the sidewalks and alleyways were hand swept by neatly dressed sanitation personnel. The mayor demanded that everything be perfect for the forthcoming celebration. The recently renovated portion of the city was being scrubbed and polished.

The municipal law enforcement division was operating round the clock to ensure safety for the dignitaries and masses of visitors expected shortly. The numerous street people, drugpushers, and other scofflaws were forced undercover as the authorities exerted pressure upon their activities. Mayor Thompson inspected his dominion daily and personally assumed control of the preparations. This was to be his moment of glory, his day in the sun. He had propagated the project with zeal from its inception to its current finale.

Political critics often accused Thompson of neglecting his other mayoral responsibilities and obligations, but the press and business community fully supported his priority. Widely acclaimed as the Thompson Project, the endeavor's progress was closely followed by practically every urban planner, municipal official, and architect throughout the world. Government administrators and officials scrutinized the undertaking in hopes of solving and eliminating city plights within their particular jurisdiction.

The major roadways leading into the city were repaired and repaved. Bridges were painted and resurfaced as every aspect was primed for the big event. Store owners were encouraged to glamorize their shop exteriors and to keep the window displays as attractive and professional as possible. The city council passed various resolutions to promote neighborhood beautification contests, to encourage civilian participation, and to select a song to publicize and honor the milestone.

Mayor Thompson had hand-picked the celebration's different subcommittees. Well-known entertainers, politicians, artists, and other distinguished individuals volunteered their time and energies for the extensive advertising campaign they hoped would ensure success. Television and radio coverage increased as the final date drew near. All glorified the project's impact upon the city, the country, and the world. With everything running near-perfect and on schedule, the final touches were being applied. The parade route was finalized and great care was taken to direct the procession only where desired. The mayor painstakingly plotted the course to feature the most innovative and lavish features of the legendary Thompson Project. The curbs and center lines were painted a brilliant green to symbolize the city's new beginning. To the outside world, the city was bordering on utopia.

THREE

But another section of the city was not included in the Thompson Project; Erebus was an area far beyond the green lines and towering skyscrapers. Here masses of indigent people lived away from the glamour and promise of the new city. This sector had been neglected for years by the city's maintenance departments and had deteriorated dreadfully. Streets were usually impassable, forcing most public transportation to bypass Erebus. The bulk of the residents were unemployed or unskilled laborers. Minorities were the majority and many different languages were spoken.

The fire department would not enter Erebus unless the blaze threatened neighboring, more privileged residents; most fires went unchecked. The charred residue of once huge buildings dotted the region, serving as a perpetual warning to those restricted within its perimeter.

Likewise, the police only responded to extreme violence. It took a riot to summon barrages of patrols, who quickly and brutally restored law and order.

Mayor Thompson regrettably acknowledged Erebus' existence, but constantly managed to channel funds to other parts of the city.

Whenever questioned about conditions there, he would articulately circumvent the plight of Erebus' residents. Compared to the remainder of the city, Erebus was insignificant; nevertheless, the sector remained a thorn in Mayor Thompson's side.

It was therefore understandable why the city's celebration avoided Erebus; any attempt to visit there by reporters was discouraged. Taxis were officially ordered not to enter Erebus during the forthcoming events.

Many Erebus residents lived in high-rise apartments. Constructed decades before, they were home to many of the city's senior citizens. Only when the elderly occupants died or moved, did space become available. Though not elite by any means, the lodgings were the best location to live within Erebus. Those not living in apartments sought shelter in the many alleys, vacant lots, or unoccupied shells of buildings.

With a mediocre school system and the lack of police security characterizing Erebus' general decay, youth gangs roamed at will and terrorized the local residents. Fighting between The Zips and The Dogs was commonplace; most of these conflicts were territorial or drug-related and usually resulted in serious injuries. The hatred among the gangs made safe travel almost impossible.

Despite all these hardships, many outstanding families still inhabited Erebus. Because of extenuating financial circumstances, many could not or would not leave their homes. After living in one place for so long, change had proven difficult. This was especially true for the sector's elderly population.

FOUR

Annette London gently nudged her husband's arm. "Come on, sleepyhead, it's time to get up!"

Stirring from sleep, Lenny stretched his arms high overhead and then rested his eyes upon his bride of forty years. "What time is it?"

"It is 10:00 a.m. We have to get ready to go shopping," she replied.

"Yes, I forgot. I will get up right away." They dressed, then waited nervously. Shortly thereafter, a gentle tapping was heard on the door. Lenny peeked through the tiny security peephole. "Who is it?"

"It's Tess and Jake, open the door," Annette urged. Lenny checked once more and then unlocked the four huge deadbolts that secured him and Annette from Erebus' unpredictable world. After relocking the many bolts behind them, the four seniors turned down the hallway to pick up several more couples. They had long since learned that traveling in large groups to the various stores lessened the chances of attack. Safety in numbers was a tactic they employed to survive; citizens depended tremendously on one another for company and support. By the time they had left the building, the troop totaled more than twenty-five. They made their way along the main thoroughfare and within ten minutes reached their destination.

Once inside the grocery store, they broke ranks and divided into several smaller groups. They purchased their goods and swiftly returned to the safety of the apartment complex. Though the building employed ten security guards, the elderly residents still felt vulnerable. Only when all had returned to their individual apartments did everyone feel more at ease.

The Londons unpacked their groceries, then Lenny read the newspaper while Annette knit a sweater for her newest grandchild. "I can't believe all the excitement over Mayor Thompson's project," remarked Lenny.

"You would think someone would help out *this* area sometime," replied Annette.

"You must be kidding. Thompson probably doesn't even know this part of the city exists."

"Can you imagine if some reporter did a story on Erebus?" said Annette. They both laughed.

Later that day, Tess and Jake returned, and the four friends played several games of bridge. Though their lives were constantly in jeopardy, most senior citizens attempted to ignore this fact, and manage a somewhat normal existence.

FIVE

Every aspect of Alice Trumbel's existence had been altered by the city's pending celebration. Her usual daytime schedule had to be rearranged. Pressure from the police and other officials was relentless. Mayor Thompson's decree was being followed to the letter and every negative presence was being driven from the city.

Every time Alice rested on a bench, an official immediately enforced the mayor's orders. Instead of arguing or demanding her rights, she gathered her belongings and walked away. As fatigued as she was, Alice followed the officers' mandates. Occasionally, she would locate an inconspicuous alley and hide in a doorway or behind a dumpster. There, safe from the constant intimidation, she rested.

Walking up Broadway, Alice liked to admire the lovely decorations that filled the many storefronts. She beamed at the adornments; each seemed to rekindle different memories. Dragging her cart behind her, she watched as patrons dashed from store to store in quest of their materialistic goals. Their reactions were generally the same toward the elderly bag lady: annoyance, distrust, or disdain. At first, these responses bothered Alice, but in time, the pain lessened. She could never understand them; after all, she never would hurt or offend any other living soul.

Reaching into her cart, she soon realized her food supply was running low. After eating sparingly, she repacked the tiny morsels and returned to the main street. At a restaurant, she rummaged through the garbage. This was no time for self-esteem or pride; her very existence depended on finding something to eat. Luckily, Alice was not only able to satisfy her hunger, but also managed to restock her dwindling reserve. A voice from behind startled her, "What are you doing there?"

Turning around, she found an especially young officer.

"I was just looking for something to—" she began.

"Look, you know the mayor's orders. I don't want to be forced to take you in, so just get going."

"I was hungry and—"

"I said to get going!" Alice glumly lumbered out of the alleyway and uptown.

"It's not fair," she uttered softly. "I was not doing anything wrong. Why are they doing this to me?" Her desire to sleep was increasing, but since the park patrols had been increased, another location would have to be found. Moving ever so slowly, she entered a side street and spied a huge pile of empty cartons. Maneuvering to the rear, she lay on the cold cement. With her old, torn coat pulled tightly about her body, Alice soon fell asleep.

Several hours later, she awoke refreshed; after gathering her few precious possessions, she forged ahead. As the days passed and the celebration drew closer, things became even harder for Alice. Restaurants were no longer permitted to keep their garbage outside, thus terminating her primary source of food. The police permitted no one to loiter on the streets. Recognizing things would probably be getting worse, Alice set out for the city's women's shelter. Though she hated it profoundly, the sanctuary could provide her with a temporary answer. Once the events were over, she prayed everything would return to normal.

The notice on the door told the entire story:

CLOSED FOR THE NEXT SIXTY DAYS. SHOULD YOU REQUIRE ASSISTANCE, PLEASE GO TO THE WOMEN'S SHELTER LOCATED AT 1120 SOUTHEASTERN PARKWAY, EREBUS.

"Erebus!" Alice exclaimed aloud. "My God, of all places, not there!" Shaking her head with disgust, she walked in an easterly direction. She resolved to stick it out a little longer. If pressed she could always resort to the women's shelter at Erebus. Alice noticed along her travels that fewer street people were about. She surmised the surge of pressure had been too great for most, causing the majority to retreat to Erebus. Using the newly painted green lines as her guide, she followed the course along the city's streets and avenues. She gaped at the gigantic, spotless buildings that filled the sky, and marveled at the innovative displays being erected along the parade's route. No matter where she traveled, the police harassed her and insisted she move from that portion of the city. Despite all the animosity, Alice refused to retreat into the community's inner depths.

S I X

"Lenny, come to the phone, it's Karen," Annette called out.

Picking up the extension, Lenny answered, "Hello, Karen, is that you?" Karen and Susan were the Londons' daughters.

"Yes, Daddy, it's really me," she acknowledged. "Frank and I were wondering if the two of you would like to come up for a few days?"

"I'm not sure, Karen. What do you think, Annette?"

"Well, we have plans for the next few weeks..." Annette commented.

"Cancel the plans and come on up. You haven't seen your grandchildren in years and they miss you terribly," Karen begged.

"We miss them but I just don't know. It's so hard to travel from here," Lenny stalled.

"Look, we can drive you up," Frank joined the conversation. "You can stay as long as you want. Maybe you'll even consider moving here on a permanent basis."

"You've got to be kidding," quipped Lenny.

"No, we're not! Susan and I have been talking and we both fear you are not safe. That area where you live is horrible!" Karen said.

"Now let's not exaggerate," responded Lenny. "I grant you, the city has changed somewhat, but we are safe. We have an excellent security system in the building."

"That's exactly what I mean, why do you live like that?"

"This is our home, Karen. We have lived here for over thirty-eight years and we stay because your mother and I want to remain here. You have your home and we have ours."

Karen relented. "I'm not trying to start an argument, it's just that Susan and I are upset. After all, you are our parents."

"That is true, but the fact remains your mother and I will leave if we want to go and not because the two of you feel it is no longer safe. How could we leave all our friends after all these years?"

Karen finally asked, "Well, what about the visit?"

Trying to ease the conversation, Annette quickly said, "Why don't we wait until the celebration is over? Then the traffic and the congestion will be less. I think it would do us some good to get away from here for a few days, and besides we'd love to spend some time with our grandchildren. By the way, can we speak to them?"

"Yes, Mother, I'll get them right away..." They talked for several more minutes and then hung up.

"Lenny, why are you so opposed to our moving? Karen is right, you know, this area is dangerous," Annette remarked.

"I didn't want to scare her, that's all. Why don't we plan on going up after Thompson has his big affair; then we can look the area over."

She kissed him on the cheek. "Thank you, my darling."

"Perhaps we could even find a place as nice as this," he jested.

"That won't be hard! We *would* be able to see the kids more often."

"You're right, perhaps we should have done it years ago. This is certainly no way to live."

"I will call Karen tomorrow and set a date for the visit." As they were leaving, the couple methodically checked their window locks and then locked the front door behind them. Together, they walked down the hallway to Michael's apartment. After knocking and iden-tifying themselves, their friend unbolted his door and ushered them into his flat. For the rest of the day, they watched television and played cards.

S E V E N

In the cellar of a burnt-out building, The Zips were celebrating the past few weeks' conquests. With every opposing gang currently eliminated—except for The Dogs—they could now concentrate fully on that quest. Their losses had been heavy; however the victories were sweet. With their latest triumph, the horde now controlled about half of Erebus and greedily eyed the remainder.

While the chieftains and attack commanders secretly met elsewhere, hundreds of members feasted. Drugs and alcohol elevated the party's levity and soon Erebus echoed with blaring music and merriment. With no police force assigned, this party promised to continue until it exhausted itself. No resident living nearby dared complain or attempt to silence the exhilaration.

E I G H T

A lone figure silently made his way amidst the rubble. Weaving among the shadows, he skillfully maneuvered until he reached his desired location. Knowing one false move could mean certain death, he calculated his next course of action. Just as he was about to sneak around a small pile of scorched lumber, three Zips wrestled him to the ground. Though drunk, they easily subdued his smaller body. Holding a knife to the stranger's throat, the largest gang member sneered, "Well look what I found: a damn Dog."

"Kill the pig!" shouted another.

"Yeah, let me do it," interjected the third.

Gasping for breath, the fallen enemy said, "I've come in peace, I got a message for Dagger."

Easing his grasp slightly, the largest Zip asked, "You'd better talk fast or I'll put this knife between your eyes."

"I was sent by Brutus. I got a message for Dagger."

"What is it?"

"I can only give it to Dagger. I was told not to tell anyone else."

"Tell me or I'll cut off an ear," threatened the leader.

"I can't. It's only for Dagger." The large one was about to kill his hostage, before his two companions pulled him away.

"What if he's telling the truth? Suppose he's really got a message for Dagger?"

"What happens if he doesn't?"

"Then you can kill him later." Agreeing, they crudely pulled their victim to his feet.

"You'd better not be lying or I'll kill you myself—and I guarantee it will be painful and slow." The captive did not respond, but remained silent as he was yanked and shoved along the way. Approaching a darkened building, the largest hood again spoke. "Keep him here; I'll be right back. If he tries to get away, cut his throat!" Moving to the side door, he hesitated momentarily, and then knocked.

After two more raps, the door opened a slit and a voice asked, "Who's there?"

"It's Big Gene."

"What are you doing here?"

"We captured a Dog."

"So kill him! We're busy."

"He says he's got a message for Dagger."

"A message? From who?"

"He says it's from Brutus."

"Brutus?"

"Yeah."

"Wait a minute, I'll be right back." The door closed, leaving Big Gene alone in the dark. He stood only for a few minutes; the door reopened and the same voice spoke, "Dagger wants to see him. Bring him in."

Maneuvering the Dog inside, they guarded him closely as the Zip's hierarchy moved in for a closer look. Dagger stared menacingly at the leather-covered captive. "So, Dog, what's this all about?"

"I got a message from Brutus."

"From Brutus? What does that pig want from me?"

"I've got no idea, I'm only here to give you the message and deliver back your answer."

"Okay, let me have it and this better be real or else I'll…"

"It is. If your friends will release my hands, I can get the message."

"They let you go when I tell them to and not before. Just tell me where it is."

"Open my shirt."

The huge leader strutted forward and grabbed the front of the fabric. He pulled harshly, tearing the cloth like paper. Inside was a sealed piece of paper. Dagger took the letter and opened it up. He stared at the page for a moment and then handed it back to the victim. "Read it!"

"But it's supposed to be a secret. I'm not supposed to know it at all."

"Don't worry, chances are you won't be able to tell anyone at all," Dagger said, threatening.

Unfolding the note, the victim loudly read its message: "Dagger, since there are only two gangs left, why not make peace instead of fighting? We can rule the whole region. Instead of killing ourselves, let's protect what we have and divide the rest between our two gangs. If you say no, then the war could last a long time. Then both of our gangs suffer. Elk will bring back your answer. If anything happens to him, then we will declare war and fight you until only one gang is left!"

Elk gingerly handed the paper back to Dagger who looked at his fellow members. "Keep him here until we get back. If he tries anything, just break his arms; but don't kill him. At least, not right now." The council walked into another room. They stayed inside for over an hour. During that period, they discussed the letter and its possible consequences for their gang. A lot of what Brutus had written was true. Finally they returned.

"Take him to the edge of our camp and let him go. Tell Brutus I want to talk to him. The meeting place must be neutral and no funny stuff."

"I'll give him your message," Elk replied as he was led toward his own gang's territory.

N I N E

A series of sirens drew the uniformed forces like flies to sugar. Alice sat in a small park. With no one to badger her, she used this precious time to relax as tots romped in a tiny playground.

Closing her eyes momentarily, Alice recalled her past. Her childhood was filled with warm memories. Being raised in the country afforded her the luxury of fresh air and a wholesome upbringing. As an only child, she was continually given every opportunity by her parents. She attended a private boarding school and then went on to an Ivy League university. After graduating with honors, she ventured to the city for her first job.

Her climb to success was unparalleled as she scrambled up the corporate chain. After meeting Stephen, the two became inseparable. Their courtship lasted seven years, but was abruptly terminated when Alice found her lover in a compromising situation with his secretary. Despite his attempts to reconcile their relationship, she repelled every gesture and fell quickly into a long, grievous depression. Nothing seemed to have any value or meaning and Alice hastily retreated from the world she had known. The tragic news of her parents' accidental death turned Alice to alcohol and drugs as a means of escape.

From there, her career plummeted; it was only a matter of time before she was fired. Unable to support herself or her habits, she eventually had no recourse but to turn to the streets. There, she used any method to obtain money. For three years she allowed herself to be exploited by anyone willing to pay for services rendered.

Incarceration was inevitable. While at the city's Women's House of Detention, both her drug and drinking problems were painfully ended. The cost was exceedingly high on Alice's body and left her emotionally scarred for life. Besides being physically abused by the other inmates, frequent beatings and psychological harassment by the prison staff were common. In many ways, her release from the institution was lifesaving. Alice surmised her very existence would have ended quickly if she had remained in jail much longer. Suicide would have been inescapable.

A light tap against her leg awakened her from her mesmerized recollection. Looking to the ground, she saw a red and white ball. After picking it up, she stared at its brightly colored composition.

"I want my ball!" A voice startled Alice. The words were repeated. Looking downward again, the old woman's eyes settled upon a small child; she guessed the girl was about six years old and judging from her appearance, the tot came from a financially comfortable family.

"Would you please give my daughter her ball?" an adult voice yelled from across the park. Alice observed a meticulously dressed woman approaching her. "I said, please give the ball back to my daughter." Out of fear, Alice clutched the ball to her chest. "If you do not give my child back her ball, I will be forced to call the police."

The elderly woman trembled slowly extended her hand outward. Because of her nervousness, her hand shook and the brightly colored ball dropped downward. The child quickly snatched the sphere and raced to her mother's side.

The younger woman glared at Alice and spoke to her child, "I don't understand why they allow that kind of person here at all. I thought Mayor Thompson was cleaning up the city!" She grabbed her daughter's hand and moved her swiftly away from the bag lady. Alice did not verbally respond, but humbly watched as the two people exited the park. A few tears flowed from the corner of each eye as her present status was again realized.

Throughout the night she clutched her few possessions, hiding behind a park dumpster. Finally the sun glistened on the surrounding glass structures. Alice gazed once more at the serene park. She meandered to the avenue in quest of a morning meal.

T E N

Because of their distrust and hatred, a neutral site had to be agreed upon by the two gang leaders. A city park outside of Erebus was designated as the perfect spot. All, of course, would be unarmed and willing to declare a temporary peace. An early Sunday morning was selected; both the public and the police would least expect any sort of confrontation. With the city at rest, the encounter could be held without distraction. Days before the meeting, both gangs avoided one another. As ordered by the two chieftains, crimes and other activities continued, but they were kept to a minimum.

The local residents were perplexed about the sudden decrease of serious gang activities; yet everyone sensed something big was about to occur. The senior citizens were the most pleased because the hiatus permitted them to function without constant apprehension. Lenny and Annette went shopping alone for the first time in years. The couple strolled down the street stopping to talk to their neighbors and friends. Instead of being forced to remain indoors, elderly residents sat on wooden benches, freely enjoying one another's company.

A hard rain fell on the city that Sunday. Wind and water lashed against the concrete structures. Lightning flashed boldly across the skies as the earsplitting sound of thunder vibrated the earth below. Because of the storm's ferocity, most of the city's citizens and support services chose to remain indoors. Luckily, Alice was able to find shelter in a deserted building. From her dry location, she watched as the squall attacked the Thompson Project; she prayed it would change the mayor's viewpoint toward her and the thousands of other homeless persons.

ELEVEN

At the designated hour, eight forms sauntered into the park. Four entered from one end while the other group arrived from another. Despite the storm, each pack silently progressed. They simultaneously reached the selected spot. No one moved or spoke as the tension increased.

Finally Dagger broke the quiet: "Come on, let's go someplace else. We can't talk here." Everyone followed as Dagger led them toward a nearby maintenance shack. He gestured, and his three comrades easily gained entrance through the locked door. Once inside, Dagger withdrew several battery-operated lanterns from beneath his studded leather jacket. He and the other members of his gang gazed at their hated adversaries, then held their hands high overhead. "Like we said, we've got no weapons. Search us if you want," offered Dagger.

"We don't have any either. Put your arms down and let's get this started!" responded Brutus.

The eight youths squatted on the concrete floor and waited for one side to begin. Brutus took the lead, "Look, our two gangs are the strongest in the whole city. It makes no sense to fight among ourselves. If we do, we are the only ones to get hurt."

"Yeah, we should make a truce of some kind," answered Dagger. The two maintained a steady discourse as their battle commanders listened intently. Occasionally the bystanders would interject a comment, but the bulk of the conversation was shared by the leaders. They discussed their gangs' modes of operation. Through the dialogue they quickly realized they had a great deal in common. After awhile, the leaders and their warriors relaxed and it became apparent some sort of agreement would be consecrated. The storm raged outside the small shelter, but inside the former enemies were finalizing a peaceful agreement.

Both gangs categorically agreed they should merge. A governing council would be formed by the eight present as well as one more member from each gang. The ten councilmen would rule the four hundred members, with ultimate control shared jointly by Brutus and Dagger. Task forces were to be established; they would develop policies on drug trafficking, prostitution, and other pertinent issues. The last item on the agenda was to decide on a name for the newly formed gang. Every person present voiced several suggestions, but none was agreeable to both factions.

Brutus then suggested, "What about Zidos?"

"How did you get that?" laughed one of his own members.

"I took letters from our previous names," answered Brutus.

"I like the idea," stated Dagger.

"The name isn't the important thing; it's the unity of the gang," explained Brutus. "We can call ourselves anything we want, but the way we rule and carry out our work is critical. We have to have a strong group."

"I agree and think the name Zidos is good," said Dagger. A vote followed and everyone shook on the new deal. The two leaders tentatively shook hands. The groups were now united into one central organization. The eight youths mingled for a few more minutes then decided to terminate their meeting. They left the park together, and returned to their individual headquarters. Within the next few days, final plans were completed and the actual merging process began. The Zidos were fully integrated over the next two weeks.

TWELVE

With only three more days before the opening ceremonies, Mayor Thompson called for a news conference. Every available reporter was at the meeting. The mayor sat at the head table surrounded by the city council, committee members, and other officials. He waited for absolute silence before speaking from the podium. After testing the microphone, he addressed the gathering: "Ladies and gentlemen of the press, I would like to thank all of you for coming this afternoon. I have called this conference to give you a glimpse of my, or should I say the city's, next project."

He waited for the mumbling to stop and continued, "Before I go on, I would first like to introduce those sitting at the head table. After the introductions, please feel free to ask any questions you might have." As the last name was announced, media hands shot up. The mayor pointed to a female reporter seated in the front row. "Ms. Darrow, what is your question?" The mayor selected her because she was a great supporter of his project.

"Thank you, Mr. Mayor. I would like to know if the Thompson Project will be completed on time."

"It appears everything is right on schedule. I have personally assumed control of this final phase and we should be finished within the next day or two." Joking, Thompson added, "Only the last green line has to be painted."

Several out-of-state reporters asked questions concerning the logistics and schedule of the forthcoming parade. The mayor easily responded to every question. With the news media in full force, Mayor Thompson wanted no errors or slip-ups by anyone under his charge. He used his political charisma to captivate his audience— and to restrict the inquiries to topics he felt appropriate for the day's meeting.

"Mr. Mayor, could you tell us why there is such a recent push to rid our streets of undesirables? Isn't there a more humanitarian way to deal with the city's homeless and prostitution problems?"

Hesitating, the mayor answered, "As you know, many essential aspects compose the Thompson Project. Besides the rebuilding phase of the plan, we want to ensure that every citizen of our city is safe from the criminal element. We are enforcing this aspect. We will no longer tolerate street criminals in our city. Under the direction of Police Commissioner Sandy Thomas, this goal is being accomplished."

"What about the homeless?" the same reporter repeated.

"They are well cared for by the Department of Human Concerns. We take great pride, as a city, in helping our less fortunate citizens."

"Mr. Mayor, why are all of the city's homeless shelters closed within the Thompson Project's sector?" another reporter persisted.

The mayor delegated his commissioner to answer the inquiry. Nervously, Jack Glass addressed the audience. "Your statement is not accurate. The seven shelters of which you speak have been closed only temporarily. All will be reopened shortly; in the meantime, those requiring assistance are being directed to our city's ten other shelters."

"Why are most of these people being diverted to Erebus?" a third reporter asked.

Jack floundered for a moment, looking to the mayor for help. Noting the weakness, the city's chief executive swiftly assumed control. "I ordered the action because of the increased activity within certain sectors of our city. Many crucial human services had to be redirected to other shelters. Several shelters are currently under reconstruction and therefore, cannot be open. Please remember, however, that all our shelters are well maintained and fully serving our needy."

"Again I ask, why are they being sent to Erebus? We all know of its problems."

"Mr. Johanson, I am not sure what exactly you are speaking about, but I would like to announce several new undertakings by this administration. We are determined to clean up the entire city and we mean every section, including Erebus. Right now, our maintenance department is planning to open any closed streets or roadways. Public transportation will be restored to every resident of our entire city, not just to a select few. I welcome any of you to speak to our commissioners concerning this matter after the meeting."

Mayor Thompson's hopes of changing the subject were quickly dimmed by the next question from the press: "What about the high crime rate? What will be done to curb this?"

"Police Commissioner Thomas and I are fully aware of this problem and as of today are committed to the reduction of all crime within our city. This includes Erebus. Right now, the police department is increasing its patrols."

"What about the youth gangs common to the inner city?"

"The authorities are making great strides in policing that region and a concerted effort will eradicate each and every hoodlum from our streets. Crime will be a thing of the past. I would like to get on with the topic of the forthcoming waterfront projects...."

Mayor Thompson maneuvered the discussion back to his agenda. At the close, he demanded that his commissioners meet him for an emergency session. Once the visitors and reporters had left, he addressed his colleagues. "I am sick and tired of hearing about

Erebus! Get several men over there, and start cleaning up some of the roads. We can bring those workers back after the celebration, but for now, let's make it look good."

Turning to his public relations advisor, the mayor continued, "Get a few articles and news shots on the work being done. Let's not go overboard, but make it look impressive." Speaking next to his other commissioners, he went on, "I want police patrols dispatched immediately to Erebus; have them make a few arrests. Go after some gang members and bust their leaders for anything. You can always find something! Get the fire department to send in its inspectors and let them work on some token jobs. I want the media to be fully aware of these happenings and especially, let them know of arrests. Are there any questions?"

No one spoke or challenged Thompson's authority. All knew what was expected and the reasons. As political professionals, their task was to obey.

THIRTEEN

The warmth of the new day's sun caressed Alice's fatigued body. Because she slept in cramped quarters, her limbs literally ached. Looking around, she scanned for anything of value to her. Stretching, she allowed herself the luxury of a slow start. The past few weeks had been a nightmare and she looked forward to the culmination of the city's festivities. Perhaps, she thought, life would return to normal for her and the rest of the street people.

In a broken mirror, she saw her reflection. Staring at the alien face in the glass, she tried to rationalize the series of events that had led her to this situation. Thoughts of her childhood, college days, and work filtered through her mind. She cursed her ex-lover and hated him for the wrongs he had inflicted. And she sank into a deep sorrow over the loss of her parents.

Bringing a hand up she examined the wrinkled, weather-beaten skin. Her bloodshot eyes revealed her restless plight and her clothes manifested her lack of personal hygiene. She inwardly knew there was no way back or more importantly, no one to return to. She gathered her belongings and left the building.

The new day brought many surprises. She had heard so many

horror stories about Erebus that the sight of blue uniforms was an enigma. Walking along the main boulevard, she watched as the city's maintenance department rehabilitated several of the streets. In a short time, patrol cars and buses cruised around. To her surprise the police left her alone. Dragging her cart, Alice watched as teams of inspectors investigated the multitude of annihilated buildings. They scurried about the structures and dictated reports. All were shocked by the sector's deplorable conditions.

With no one to bother her, Alice was content fending for her needs. Her only problem was competing with the many other street people who had been forced to relocate to Erebus. All had similar requirements, and with such a limited supply of food, everyone competed for nourishment.

The city's shelters were overcrowded and unable to adequately care for all those needing help.

Reporters ranged through Erebus taking pictures of the devastated landscape. Interviews with local business persons and citizens unveiled how the city's disgrace had been hidden for years. Dramatic media stories of devastating poverty soon overshadowed the Thompson Project and public attention was diverted toward the residents of Erebus.

FOURTEEN

The mayor was livid. He called an emergency meeting of his staff. He and his political advisors had miscalculated the public's reaction to neglected poverty. Throwing the day's newspapers across the room, he demanded to know what had gone wrong. A strategy error—his own—was now undermining Thompson's plan and political goals. Finally after ranting and raving, the mayor plopped heavily in his chair and sought assistance. "What are we going to do?"

Admonitions and recommendations flew across the table. Everyone voiced their opinion but none could adequately define a solution to bury the problem. After hours of tiresome debate, Mayor Thompson turned to his public relations advisor. "Make an announcement tomorrow that the mayor's office has designated the rehabilitation of Erebus as Phase Two of the Thompson Project. We, the political arm of our city, are appalled at the sector's condition and are making it a top priority on our agenda. Also alert the media that the waterfront project will be started after this cleanup is finished. Does anyone have any questions?"

Getting no response, he added, "I don't care how you do it, but I want total coverage on the Thompson Project. I have worked too hard and too long on this undertaking to let it get second billing. Now let's get the media's attention back where it belongs."

STANLEY L. ALPERT

FIFTEEN

Lenny and his friend Jake stood outside the apartment building. "Did you hear the announcement by the mayor's PR advisor?" asked Lenny.

"Yes, do you think they are really going to improve Erebus?" inquired Jake.

"I think it will happen. Some of the streets have been reopened and I have seen more police around the neighborhood. In fact, a couple of days ago was the last time any hooligans bothered any of us," Lenny offered.

"I guess you're right. It certainly took enough time."

"Are you going to the celebration?" asked Jake.

"No, we are going to watch it on television. Why don't the two of you join us?" Lenny suggested.

"I'll let you know, but it sounds like fun."

"Let's have a little party of our own. It's been such a long time since any of us had anything to celebrate. Let's have a New Erebus party."

"An excellent idea. I'll call you later to finalize plans," Jake promised.

38

The two men returned to their apartments. Lenny unlocked his door and looked for Annette, "Hello, honey, I'm home."

"I'll be right out." Lenny walked into their bedroom and looked lovingly at his wife as she brushed her hair. He still worshipped her after all these years; he had dedicated his life to her happiness. Moving to her side, he pulled her close, gently rubbing her back.

"To what do I owe this attention?" she softly said. "Remember, you're not a kid anymore."

"I am just so glad; it appears our neighborhood is going to improve and we will not have to move."

"Do you think it will really happen?" asked Annette.

"Absolutely. Every day changes are being made. Today, I saw ten policemen on the avenue. Can you believe it? Ten!"

"That's more than we've seen in years," remarked Annette.

"You're right and that's why I am so excited. Perhaps we can start living again…how would you like to take a walk to the park today?"

"To the park? We have not been there in years. Do you think it is safe?"

"Why not? With all the police around, no one will bother us. Besides, I'd like to see if the place has changed," said Lenny.

She nervously agreed. He asked her about the celebration party and she thought it was a marvelous idea. *Yes,* Lenny thought, *things would certainly be different.*

Mayor Thompson's attention to Erebus was welcomed by the majority of its citizens. The announcement of Phase Two of the Thompson Project guaranteed a revitalization of the last remaining sector. Businesses would begin to prosper as real estate developers and speculators purchased property.

The Zidos were stunned by the announcement. Every aspect of their lifestyle was jeopardized. Brutus and Dagger met frequently, often in emergency sessions, to determine the gang's best course. The increase of police presence caused a rapid decline in their prostitution and drug businesses. With loss of revenue, other alternatives had to be explored. Frequent raids and numerous arrests by law enforcement agencies demoralized even their strongest and most dedicated members. The gang was no longer free to roam and the enforcement network concentrated on all their illegal enterprises. Frustration intensified as the gang's leadership sought answers to the dilemmas. With nowhere else to relocate, Erebus was their last stronghold and they vowed not to give it up without a fight.

Dagger suggested sabotaging the city's celebrations, but Brutus quickly vetoed. The Zidos' strength was not potent enough to challenge the entire city's police force. However, Brutus agreed some retaliation was in order. After the gaiety and festivity had passed then they would get even.

S I X T E E N

Alice couldn't have been more pleased. Without the harassment of the police and her freedom restored, she fulfilled her limited needs. Her latest windfall was the discovery of a deserted alley. Blocked at one end by fallen debris, the other entrance opened onto a small side street. Other than a weekly pickup by the municipal sanitation department, nothing else stirred. Alice constructed a temporary shelter from scattered rubble that filled the alley. Though makeshift and crude, it more than adequately provided her with cover. With a reliable food supply close by, she enjoyed her new arrangement.

By diverting several waterspouts, she was able to fabricate an impromptu shower. Using a tiny remnant of soap she had salvaged, she washed away the grime. The cold water felt good as she cleansed her filthy body. After washing her long, unruly hair, she washed her only clothing. Hidden within her shelter she waited for everything to dry. Hours later Alice dressed and after concealing her few possessions, she walked along the avenue. With an air of renewal she spoke freely with others along the way.

SEVENTEEN

Lenny and Annette wandered down the street. Hand in hand, they window-shopped outside stores. They noticed many more pedestrians. The elder population took advantage of their new freedom. Tension has eased and most people smiled as they passed. Cars and buses traversed the newly reopened streets, making transportation to other city boroughs possible. Lenny and Annette idly proposed trips to museums and other points of interest. They vowed once the Thompson Project celebrations were over, their ventures out of Erebus would commence.

At last the couple approached the park. Though littered and unkempt, the oasis still presented a glimpse of nature to apartment dwellers. Resting on a wooden bench, they watched as a middle-aged bag lady walked nearby. Though her clothes were stained and wrinkled, Annette and Lenny could see they had been recently cleaned.

"I feel sorry for her," stated Annette.

"I do too," her husband agreed. "But remember, most of them prefer to live that way."

"It's just that she looks so deprived of everyday things," mused Annette.

"I know what you mean but we can't change the world," Lenny reminded her.

"You're right, my dear, as usual."

They spent a few hours strolling and watching the trees and grass wave in the gentle breeze. Others ventured into the park. Some fed the pigeons and squirrels; others were content to luxuriate in the tiny nature preserve. Lenny and Annette at last started their trek home. Lulled from the peaceful day, neither noticed the two figures following at a distance.

The sound of running feet caused both to turn. A second later, Lenny was knocked to the ground by a jolt from behind. The two Zidos easily overpowered their victims and seized the quarry. Annette was shoved harshly forward as a youth grabbed her bag. She resisted and shouted. Lenny tried to help his wife, but was again shoved to the pavement by the taller of the two gang members.

A deafening shot caused them all to freeze. Within seconds three officers surrounded the group. They assisted the Londons to their feet and restrained and handcuffed the thieves. The officers wrote details of the assault and then wrestled the two Zidos into a waiting car.

"Will you come to the station to formally charge these two if necessary?"

Lenny turned to his bruised wife, then said adamantly, "Yes, I will."

"Good, I am not sure it will be necessary, but I want to make sure we rid the streets of trash like this." Turning to his partner, he said, "Why don't you walk these fine people to their home and we'll drag these two in for questioning."

The car drove off and the young officer escorted the Londons to their apartment. Watching the entire incident were Brutus and several other gang members. Turning to one of his colleagues, he said, "Follow them and find out where they live. Be careful; don't let them know you're there." After he had acquired the desired address, the young Zido returned to their headquarters to report.

EIGHTEEN

"Lenny, I'm busy ,would you get the phone?" asked Annette.

He picked up the receiver but got no response to his hello. "Hello, is anyone there?" Lenny repeated.

"Drop the charges or you'll pay dearly." A click told Lenny the calling party had hung up. Replacing the phone on its cradle, he remained silent for a few moments.

"Who was it, dear?" Annette called from the other room.

Hesitating, Lenny replied, "Just a wrong number. They wanted another party."

Lenny was exceptionally quiet for the next couple of hours.

"Are you feeling okay? You're not yourself," asked Annette.

"I'm fine," Lenny replied bluntly.

"Perhaps we should go see Dr. Weiss. Maybe you were hurt during the robbery."

"Stop worrying. I feel just fine. Call Jake and let's make plans for our party—" Before Lenny could say another word the phone rang again. Grabbing it, he listened. "You'll be sorry if you don't drop the charges," came a threatening voice from the other end.

Lenny spoke through clenched teeth, "Look, I don't know who

you are, but stop threatening me." Another click signified the caller had hung up.

"What is it?" asked Annette. "Who called?"

"Nothing," he said softly. "It was just a prank call."

"Are you telling me the truth?" asked Annette, who had heard his tone.

"Yes, now let's go to Jake's and prepare for this Thompson Project celebration," Lenny suggested, trying to leave the phone call behind.

Unlocking their door, the couple noticed a folded piece of paper attached to their peephole. Lenny opened the paper and silently read the contents. "What is it?" asked Annette. He did not respond and instead reluctantly handed her the letter.

Annette read the threat and turned to her husband, "Who did this?" He shrugged his shoulders. "Were the phone calls the same?" she asked.

He whispered, "Yes."

Annette began to comprehend the gravity. "My God! What should we do?"

"Nothing yet. Let's just see what happens." The phone rang again, causing both to jump.

"Let me answer it," Annette's fear had transformed to anger.

"No," Lenny said. "Let it ring. Come. Let's go."

They explained the harrowing events to their friends and listened as everyone expressed their opinion. They concurred that if the calls persisted, the authorities would have to be notified. Trying to forget the trauma of the attempted robbery and subsequent threats, the group played several rubbers of bridge and then ate supper. By 10 p.m. Lenny and Annette returned to their apartment.

The phone rang within a few minutes of their return. Annette picked up the receiver and listened. "If you don't drop the charges, you'll regret it."

"I don't know who you are, but if you don't stop this immediately, I will report you to the police."

"If you and your husband do not drop the charges against my friends, both of you are dead!"

Shaking and desperate, Annette shouted into the receiver, "Why can't you leave us alone?" Turning to Lenny she said, "Please call the police and drop the charges. We don't need this. Please!"

Lenny dialed the local precinct. The phone rang for the longest time before a voice finally answered.

"Hello, this is the twenty-first precinct. Sergeant Mallery speaking."

"This is Lenny London and I wish to drop charges against the two youths who—"

"Mr. London, may I interrupt for one minute? Because tomorrow is the city's big celebration, Mayor Thompson has ordered every available officer to the parade route. A few others and I are alone in the station. There is no way we can assist you at this time."

"But we are being threatened..."

"I understand your dilemma but I cannot send you any help. Every patrol car and extra officer is gone. Those remaining cannot leave."

"What are we supposed to do? Our lives are in danger!"

"It is common for phone threats to occur, but rarely does anything ever really happen. May I suggest that you move in with another family or friends for the next two days. Once the festivities are over, we can get to the bottom of your problem."

"But—" Lenny pleaded.

"I am sorry but I must hang up. The phones are ringing and I am alone at the switchboard. Just hold on for a few days and above all, don't panic. That is what the caller is hoping for. Just remain calm."

As Lenny placed the phone in the cradle, it rang. Lenny remained composed as he listened. "Hear me, old geezer, drop the charges or else."

Controlling his mix of fear and fury, Lenny responded, "I just spoke to the police and they said—"

"The police cannot help you. Nothing can anymore. If the

charges are not dropped by tomorrow noon, both you and your wife are going to die."

"It cannot be done by then, the officer—"

"By tomorrow at 12:00 p.m. or that's it." Click.

Lenny replaced the phone and moved cautiously to Annette. They held each other, silently wondering what to do next. Again the phone rang and Lenny ran to answer. "Look," he pleaded, "Leave us alone. I'll drop the charges. Please, just leave us alone."

"Daddy, what is going on? I have been trying to reach you all day...and what are you talking about? Charges?" the Londons' daughter Susan asked.

Lenny handed the phone to his wife, "It's Susan."

Annette took the phone. "Oh, Susan, I am so glad to hear your voice. Your father and I need your help."

"What happened?"

Annette related the events of the past couple of days. She told of the threatening note and calls as well as their fruitless conversation with the police. All Susan could utter was "Oh, my God." with each new twist. "What are you going to do?"

"I am not sure, but we can't stay here. Whoever is doing this knows where we live and can easily get to us at any time. I think we will stay at a friend's apartment."

"I have a better idea. Why can't we pick you up and bring both of you to our house? They don't know where we live and you can stay here until you decide how you want to handle the situation."

"Let me talk it over with your father and I will call you right back."

The couple discussed their options for a few minutes. During their conversation the phone rang several times, but neither answered it. When they reached their decision, they phoned their daughter.

After only one ring, Susan answered, "Mother? Is that you?"

"Yes."

"Thank God. We have been worried sick."

"There is no need to worry. Your father and I have decided to visit you for awhile. We'd love to see both of you and our grandchildren. Let me put your father on so he can work out the details."

Despite Susan's vigorous objections, Lenny and Annette categorically insisted the best place to meet would be away from the apartment. Under the cover of darkness, the Londons would use the back exit and go to First Avenue. There Susan and her husband would be waiting. They agreed to meet at 9 p.m. and, barring any delays, they would arrive back at Susan's home by 11 p.m.

Still concerned about their final arrangements, Susan pleaded, "Please be careful and I love both of you. Are you sure we can't come to the front door of the building?"

Fearing for his daughter's safety, Lenny answered, "Absolutely not! We will meet you there at 9 p.m."

After hanging up, they called Jake and explained their plans. He wanted to escort them to their destination, but they rejected the idea. Too many people might attract attention. "What about the security guards?" asked Jake.

"I don't trust them," replied Lenny. "After all, how did the note get on my door?"

"Please be careful," Jake admonished unnecessarily.

"Don't worry, it is only a short way to meet Susan. I'll call you once we arrive."

Annette and Lenny packed quickly, saying little. Both were apprehensive. Each took only the bare essentials and only enough for a few days. By then, this matter would probably be resolved and the couple could return to their normal lives.

They decided to turn off all the lights except for one in the bedroom. With everything ready, they waited for the designated time for their departure.

NINETEEN

Lenny and Annette turned on the television and silently watched the opening ceremonies. Mayor Thompson and the city had gone all out to show off their latest project. Interviews with famous dignitaries and politicians filled the airways. It was no wonder the Londons could not solicit police help; every celebrity was surrounded by blue uniforms.

They listened as the police commissioner took the podium and spoke of citizen safety and their new city. He used the Thompson Project as the ultimate example and demonstrated statistically the city's sharp decline in crime. Neither Lenny nor Annette commented on his speech, but listened with special interest to his references to Erebus.

As the clock struck 8:30 p.m. Lenny broke their silent vigil. "I think we should be leaving." Annette hugged him and then inspected their apartment.

"We are only going to be away for a few days, what is the big deal?" Lenny said anxiously.

"I just want to make sure everything is in place. I'd hate to come back to a dirty apartment."

He held her again, "Don't worry, everything will be fine."

She did not answer, but pulled him closer. He gathered up their two small bags and unlocked the door. A new note was attached to their doorway. "Leave it alone, we'll look at it when we come back," warned Lenny.

She nodded her assent and watched as he locked the door. After rechecking the bolt once more, they hurried to the elevator. The building was silent as they descended to the lower level. Finding no one there, they wound their way to the back door. Annette kissed Lenny once more before the couple plunged into the darkness.

Neither spoke as they strode along the rear driveway. The only sound was their footsteps, which echoed loudly among the tall apartment buildings. Reaching the street, they scanned both ways and, finding it void of movement or life, the elderly couple bravely struck out for First Avenue. They were amazed at the stillness that gripped the thoroughfare where they walked. Awkwardly carrying their suitcases, Lenny and Annette progressed toward their objective. Several of the streetlights had been repaired and their rays assisted the couple to safely maneuver. The sound of footsteps to their rear caused both to hesitate in mid-stride.

Turning around slowly, Lenny saw a group of youths. Clutching his wife's arm, they quickened their pace. Suddenly they observed another band coming toward them from ahead. With hearts pounding, they looked around. Noting an isolated alley slightly to their left, they walked to its entrance. Staring once more at the approaching gangs, Lenny and Annette stepped into the darkness.

Fear drove them ahead. As their eyes adjusted, they noticed the alleyway terminated just in front of where they stood. "Now what?" whispered Annette.

Lenny whispered back, "Let's wait and see what happens. Maybe we are just overly nervous."

They remained motionless as the footsteps drew nearer. Both groups congregated at the entrance to the alley. Suddenly flashlights beamed and more than twenty youths entered the alley. With no place to hide, Lenny and Annette stood their ground. As the lights stalked their prey, the youths quickened their pace. Annette held on tightly to her husband as the band surrounded them. No one said a word as the many beams finally conjoined on the elderly couple's faces. A gruff voice slyly said, "Well if it isn't Mr. and Mrs. London."

Lenny strained to recognize the source, but the lights made identification impossible. "I'm afraid I can't see who you are. How do you know me?"

There was silence, then one of the youths moved forward. "Lenny, did you think you could run from us?"

Terrified, Lenny replied, "Run? My wife and I were taking a walk."

"Do you always take a walk with suitcases?"

"Please let us go and I won't tell anybody about this."

"Lenny, do you think we are stupid? We gave you plenty of warning and this is what you do."

"But I called the police and told them I want to drop the charges."

"Elk is still in jail!"

"I know, they told me nothing could be done for a few days, everyone is at the celebrations."

"You had a time limit."

"I know but what am I to do? I tried!"

"That's not my problem, it's yours."

"Please let us go and I will go down to the station tomorrow and make sure your friend is released."

"How can I trust you?"

"I give you my word!"

"Your word!" Loud laughter followed. "Your word means nothing to me. Perhaps we'll just keep your wife for awhile. Let's just call it insurance."

Several of the gang moved forward. Lenny stood before Annette and shouted, "Leave her alone!" Five members quickly grabbed the old man and threw him to the ground. He struggled to get up, but was kicked repeatedly.

Brutus pulled Annette aside and pawed roughly at her. Lenny made another attempt to stand, but was struck by a blunt object. Annette struggled and managed to strike Brutus' face. His reaction was swift: He threw her to the pavement then sorely touched his chin. A trickle of blood flowed from the corner of his mouth. He tasted its flavor and then withdrew a long, pointed knife. There was no debate or discussion, he thrust the weapon deep into the elderly woman's chest.

Lenny, dazed from the blows, crawled to his wife's lifeless form. Looking upward at Brutus, he cried, "You son-of-a…" The final word never left his mouth. Dagger withdrew his knife from Lenny's neck and wiped the blood on the elderly victim's jacket.

A noise in the rear of the alley caused every gang member to turn. Lights swung in the new direction and the group moved forward. They discovered the middle-aged bag lady cowering within her makeshift shelter. They dragged her into the alley and stared at her motley body. Alice begged, but the end was quick. The last words she ever heard came from Dagger's mouth: "Kill her!"

TWENTY

The newspapers covered the city's celebration extensively. Pictures of Mayor Thompson and the other famous dignitaries graced nearly every page. Television and radio coverage was almost indistinguishable.

On the last page of the city's paper, a brief story reported the following: "In Erebus today, three bodies were discovered in a small alley. They were all brutally knifed and their bodies hidden under piles of rubble. The police refused to release the names or identities of the victims until their relatives are reached. Officials will conduct a thorough investigation and hope to make an arrest soon."

Of Sacrifice
and Gratitude

O N E

Frederick Lorins lived alone after the death of his wife Irma. The couple had been married thirty-five years. During their first five years, they had lived in a small apartment but once their first daughter Kathleen was born, they had decided to purchase a home.

On weekends, they would attempt to find a house that was financially within their limited means. It was an exhausting search, but after months of looking, they discovered a modest handyman's special. Though quite far from Fred's place of employment, the one-and-a-half-hour drive each way had been well worth his family's comfort and security.

Over the years, Fred had repaired the damaged structure and added a dormer to accommodate his growing family. The five girls required all of Irma's time and attention, especially during their younger years. Fred did the best he could to help, but free time was exceedingly limited because of his work schedule. Child-rearing was almost exclusively Irma's responsibility.

Working at the Alfred Kessler Corporation, Fred was promoted at an accelerated rate. He steadily advanced until he ultimately held a supervisory position. What he lacked from a formal education, he acquired by his intelligence and innate business sense. By retirement age, a well-endowed pension and government remunerations more than adequately covered his and Irma's financial needs.

With enough money and plenty of free time, the two eagerly planned a long and well-deserved vacation. For weeks, they visited travel agencies collecting information on several interesting places; each one seemed more enticing than the next. Pamphlets and brochures filled the living room as the two elderly explorers leafed through the piles of booklets. After much time and research, a trip to Mexico was booked. They happily anticipated their first real vacation without the children.

One month before their scheduled date of departure, Fred awoke and discovered Irma frantically gasping for breath. He attempted to calm her as she clutched her chest and then helplessly watched her go limp. Her lifeless body lay at his side as he telephoned for assistance.

Irma's death pierced the very essence of Fred's soul. Though his children tried to fill the void, none could ever replace his beloved Irma. It was to be a turning point of his life.

After canceling their vacation plans, he attempted to salvage the fragments of a once happy existence. It took months before he was able to empty the house of her clothes and personal possessions. Except for a few sentimental keepsakes, everything was removed. What his five daughters did not want, charitable organizations received. Many a night, Fred would cry himself to sleep while clutching her pillow to his chest.

Years after Irma's death, an emptiness still engulfed him and the house. He refused to socialize with any of their remaining friends and slowly became a man unto his own world. Except for his children and their families, he admitted few into his private sovereignty. Most of his time was spent puttering around the yard in good weather and doing odd projects when forced to stay inside.

With age impairing his vision and judgment, his children implored him to sell his car. After resisting for a long time, he final ly gave in and accepted dependency. Kathleen would take him shopping once a week and would transport him where and when required. Fate was dealing one cruel blow after another.

Kathleen took him for an annual checkup to his long-time family physician, Dr. Kole. It was as if his once-strong physique was deteriorating and forsaking its owner. Borderline diabetes, asthma, and rheumatoid arthritis crept into his life and took their cumulative toll. Tasks that were formerly taken for granted were now exceedingly difficult and often impossible. Television, radio, and the telephone, which he had always deplored, were now his sole links to the outside world.

T W O

Kathleen, the oldest child, married immediately after graduating high school. Since she had wed her high school sweetheart, it was only natural that they lived locally. Being the first born, she was extremely close to her family, even after marriage. A special affection was shared with her father. It was, therefore, quite instinctive and almost expected that she assume control of her father's well-being and necessities.

Kathleen's husband Harold accepted this relationship and never questioned his wife's actions. He, like Fred, was a self-made businessman. Throughout his teens, he had worked at various service stations; each experience enhanced his automotive skills. It was anticipated he would pursue this course after high school. With financial and moral support from Irma and Fred, Harold had purchased a small service station on the outskirts of town.

It was extremely difficult in the beginning, but with his acquired aptitude and the commercial and residential expansion of the region, success followed. Throughout this period, Fred gave additional monetary assistance when necessary. Never once did he expect any of the funding to be repaid.

Kathleen and Harold purchased their family home three years after the service station opened. Though modest, it filled their needs. With Harold's job requiring extensive time, raising their two sons was Kathleen's responsibility. Like Irma, she never complained and accepted her role graciously.

Her father's decline disturbed her greatly, so she catered to his every need. When shopping for her own family, she stopped by his house and took him too. She would help him pick out various items and often pay a portion of his bill. Many times, she would cook extra food and bring it to his house. Because he had been recently diagnosed as a borderline diabetic, she had been warned by Dr. Kole that appropriate nutrition was necessary to maintain her father's overall health. By cooking for him, she was assured he was eating a balanced diet.

Fred not only enjoyed their weekly jaunts, but greatly appreciated the occasional Sunday visits to her home. There he would freely converse with Kathleen, Harold, and his grandchildren. Since Harold's parents had both died when he was fairly young, his father-in-law was his only link to the prior generation. For this and other personal reasons, the elderly man was welcome in their small, but intimate home.

THREE

Deborah was the perpetual dissident of the five children. When she was in her teens, her rebellious attitude and behavior often overwhelmed her conservative parents. Though she never caused any real problems, Deborah's approach was to live and let live.

During high school, she passed without difficulty but never really utilized her potential. Despite her mediocre academic record, Fred and Irma elected to finance her college education. With trepidation, they withdrew their small savings and enrolled their second daughter at a state university. Not only did she prove a late bloomer, she applied herself beyond everyone's expectations. She graduated first in her class and was easily accepted to the country's finest law school. Her parents and family sat proudly during her college graduation ceremony as Deborah was bestowed with awards. With several scholarships and assistance from her parents, she was able to concentrate fully on her advanced education and within three short years, graduated fifth in her class from law school.

Job offers from around the country were forthcoming. Instead of responding immediately, she chose to return home for the summer to reacquaint herself with her family. This was a special time for

Fred and Irma. The union that had always been fraught with friction during her earlier years melded and by the end of the summer they enjoyed a loving relationship.

Together they evaluated her many professional opportunities, and jointly selected the one best suited to her objectives. The optimum position was located three hours away by plane; all of them realized distance might once again draw them apart. To prevent this from recurring, they made a concerted effort to maintain the relationship. Regular telephone conversations and frequent letters enhanced the love that had been kindled.

Deborah's progress was outstanding. Within a few short years, she was made a senior partner and commanded a six-figure salary. During this time, she met and married Donald Frawley. Because her husband's business was located in the same city, they purchased a luxurious penthouse between their two offices.

Deborah and Donald, despite their hectic schedules, always made a concerted effort to visit her parents. Donald was warmly accepted by her entire family and, despite their financial dissimilarity, a harmonious and loving rapport developed. After Irma's death, this attachment endured.

F O U R

Deborah's sister Vera had always been classified as an exceptional child. A freak childhood accident rendered her blind from the age of five. After consulting scores of ophthalmologists, the final verdict was a permanent loss of vision to both eyes. Fred and Irma were crushed as they absorbed the anguish along with their daughter. Realizing the public schools were not adequately equipped to handle such a unique situation, Vera was enrolled in a private academy that specialized in the visually impaired.

Each night all the children worked on their assignments; none labored as diligently as Vera. Despite her visual loss, she never gave up or felt sorry for herself. In fact, her blindness acted as an incentive to strive for the best and never settle for less. As if driven to perfection, she easily mastered the art of Braille and other functional procedures, which permitted her to lead an almost normal life. She played with her sisters and never used her visual loss as an excuse.

On weekends when Fred was home, he provided whatever assistance was necessary. Wherever the family went, Vera always went along. She worked in the gardens and, using her exceptionally developed sense of touch, took pride in caring for the young vegetables; she was able to envision many of the plants and their byproducts.

Upon graduating high school, the local blind association sponsored Vera's college education. Because of her warmth and tremendous humanitarianism, Vera's interest was special education. She enrolled at a neighboring university and graduated with honors. Throughout this time, Irma transported her to and from school daily.

During college, Vera met another blind student named Jason. They were attracted and, despite both sets of parents' reservations, the two married after graduation. Their first jobs were coincidentally at the same school. Through great hardships—perhaps because of them—their marriage was very strong.

On weekends, Fred went to their apartment and helped Vera and Jason. He was especially appreciated after the birth of their first child Timothy. The proud grandfather transported the family to various appointments and would regularly take them shopping for clothing and food.

Fred and Irma experienced fulfillment when they instructed Timothy to read and write. As the young tot grew, he often acted as the eyes desperately needed in his home. This relieved his four grandparents and permitted all to spend less time at their children's home.

Irma's death increased both Jason's and Vera's love for Fred. They understood his personal sacrifice had helped them and they vowed to assist him in any way they could. As he aged and became less mobile, the telephone was their primary means of communication. Unless a friend or relative drove them to Fred's home, visits were infrequent. Despite the distance, Vera's love never waned. Time and adversity only enhanced its magnitude.

F I V E

Beth entered the family as daughter number four. Irma and Fred had hoped to be blessed with a son, but alas, those hopes were not realized. Their biggest relief was that Beth was born in perfect health.

Though she got along with all of her sisters, a special bond grew between her and Vera. Being close in age, their relationship intensified through the years. Often, she would act as her sister's eyes during play and other activities.

Being the tomboy of the group, Beth was constantly getting into juvenile adventures and various escapades. Her knees were always bruised and scratched from climbing trees, sliding on the sidewalk, or falling during a game of tag. Rambunctious was a word commonly used by her parents to characterize her exploits. Fred and Irma enjoyed most of her pranks and appreciated her zestful approach to life.

Upon high school graduation, she lived at home and enrolled at a local junior college. Finding the work monotonous and unrewarding, she discontinued her studies and took a full-time position at a large retail business. Within a few years, she advanced to a supervisory position.

Fred was especially pleased with her success and allowed her to remain at home rent-free. Promotions continued as Beth worked herself steadily upward along the managerial and organizational structure.

Other forces soon entered her life. She encountered a young man within the company who shared her philosophies and values. Together, Benjamin and Beth formalized their plans and quit their positions. With Fred's encouragement and assistance, they opened a restaurant. Hard work and long hours paid off and after a few years, their business was breaking even.

Benjamin and Beth married one year later and continued to work together in harmony. With limited time off, the couple could not socialize or enjoy the fruits of their labor. To help the young entrepreneurs, the Lorins family volunteered their time at the restaurant.

The couple was still living in the small apartment above their business at the time of Irma's death. Beth attempted to provide solace to her father, but these connections were limited to the telephone or to his visits to the restaurant. Despite her absenteeism, Beth's devotion and affection toward her father never dwindled.

S I X

Mary Anne was born one year after Beth's arrival. She was the fifth and final child to bear the Lorins family name. Fred and Irma, at this point, had given up any hopes of having a son and accepted their large family of females.

Unlike her other sisters, Mary Anne was content remaining inside the house and amusing herself with creative activities. Being the youngest, she was pampered by her parents as well as her siblings. Though she shared a room with Vera and Beth, her preference was to be alone.

Her natural talents revealed themselves early. Fred and Irma eagerly encouraged her to pursue her creativity. For holidays and birthdays, her gifts were usually artistic crafts and stories. To further bolster this activity, Mary Anne was given private art lessons at the local craft shop.

At high school, she relentlessly strove to improve her abilities and knowledge. Upon graduation, she enrolled at a prestigious art institute. Fortunately, it was situated only blocks from Fred's office; therefore Mary Anne traveled with her father daily to classes.

No one really expected her to do as well as she did. Not only were her grades above average, but more importantly, her mastery of the canvas became renowned throughout the school. Even as a student, her works were displayed by institutions and galleries. Though only a few sold, the exposure and experience were envied by Mary Anne's fellow students.

During her senior year, she fell in love with one of her teachers. Despite her parents' objections, she left home and moved into his small loft. Hal was fifteen years her senior, but their common intrigue with painting sustained a long and lasting relationship. Upon finally finishing school, she turned her full attention to the world of art.

Within their studio, the two strove for perfection and success. For years, Hal supported Mary Anne by teaching and working odd jobs. Though cramped, they chose to remain in their apartment even after their first son David was born.

With the birth of their fourth grandson, Fred and Irma reconciled their disapproval of their daughter's choice of live-in status with Hal. Visits became more frequent and before too long, the family spent weekends at Fred and Irma's house. Little David appeared to be the cement that fused the temporarily fragmented family. Though he never admitted it, Fred was thrilled to have another grandson; he managed to spoil the little tot whenever possible.

Mary Anne and Hal never realized their financial goals; however, their contentment more than compensated for the lack of material objects. Within their small loft, existence was sweet and fulfilling.

S E V E N

The five daughters lavished their father with love and kindness. Regardless of their individual niches, each held a special affection for Fred and showed it freely. Irma understood this relationship and never complained or became jealous. "After all," she would say, "if we had had boys, then the tables would have been turned."

During the early years, Irma smiled as the five girls eagerly greeted their father every night upon his arrival from work; she was amazed at their endless pampering to fulfill Fred's every need. Of course, as they grew older, their attention dwindled somewhat, but their love always remained strong.

During their childhood each child was given specific tasks to perform around the house. Every day, Irma was assisted by someone in cleaning, cooking, and other jobs necessary to maintain the family. As one daughter left home, the others were required to pick up the extra work and not rely on Irma to do everything. Eventually, Fred purchased another car. This enabled Irma to be more independent and not rely on her husband to transport her and the children on weekends. When not working, Fred was fully dedicated to his family.

E I G H T

To relieve their father's grieving after Irma died, his daughters decided to celebrate Thanksgiving at his house. Kathleen delegated various responsibilities to each of her sisters. Having been away with Harold for a well-deserved vacation, Kathleen stopped over to her father's house the day of her return.

Opening the door, she shouted inside, "Hello, Daddy, it's me." Upon hearing no response, she walked into the kitchen and saw everything was in disarray. Dirty dishes were piled in the sink and on the counter, while half-opened food containers sat on top of the kitchen table. Shaking her head in disbelief, she walked into the dining room and discovered a similar scenario. "Daddy!" she screamed, "where are you?"

Instinctively she headed toward his bedroom. Opening the door, she saw him sitting half dressed in a chair. His room was, like all the others, cluttered. The blankets and sheets were soiled and draped haphazardly on the floor. Noticing her entrance, Fred smiled and gestured warmly with his hand.

"What happened, Daddy? What's going on?"

Puzzled, he responded, "What do you mean?"

"What do I mean? The house is a mess! What happened?"

Fred turned his gaze out the window and did not answer her question. Seeking an answer, she persisted, "Daddy, did Vera or Beth stop over?"

"I am not sure. I don't think so."

Confused, Kathleen sat on the bed and assessed her surroundings. "Daddy, are you okay?"

"Why are you asking so many questions? I feel just fine."

"But the house!"

"What about the house?"

Realizing she was getting nowhere, she picked up the phone and dialed Harold. She explained the circumstances and hung up. Kathleen then called Vera and Beth. Neither had been able to help their father during the prior week, and both assumed the other was checking on Fred. Angrily, Kathleen slammed down the phone. With tears flowing, she asked, "Daddy, are you sure you are feeling okay?"

"I feel fine! Why do you keep asking me the same question?"

She did not push the issue any further, but instead started cleaning the house. Hours later, she was joined by Harold who assisted her. Sensing his wife's frustration and distress, Harold remained silent and decided to question her later. That night, when they had finally restored a semblance of order, Kathleen and Harold returned home.

N I N E

"Fred Lorins?"

"Yes?"

"Dr. Kole will see you now."

The receptionist directed Fred and his three daughters to the doctor's office. No one spoke; all of them stared at the framed degrees and awards that filled the small office. The door swung open and a medium-height man entered. He picked up Fred's chart. Looking directly at Fred he asked, "What is wrong?"

Fred shrugged his shoulders and looked to Kathleen. "We feel our father should have a checkup," she said unfalteringly.

Dr. Kole leafed through the papers and again spoke, "You were in here last year, Fred, it is time for another physical. Why don't you go to Examination Room Three and get undressed. I'll be there in a moment."

Fred looked confused. "Come, Daddy," said Beth, "I'll take you there."

As soon as they left, Kathleen described the recent changes in his behavior and the incident she had painfully discovered at his home. Dr. Kole took several notes. "Please wait here, and I will speak to you after my examination."

Forty-five minutes later, Dr. Kole reentered his office. "I have asked nurse Berger to remain with your father while I speak to all of you."

"Is anything wrong?" questioned Kathleen.

"Let me explain what I have found. Physically, your father appears to be in the same shape he was during his last examination. His heart and vital signs are normal for a person his age. As all of you already know, he suffers from a mild case of asthma and arthritis. Both these appear to be status quo. I have performed a urinary and blood workup and should have the results within the next few days. Should anything be irregular, I will certainly advise you immediately."

He hesitated for a moment and then continued, "You know, other changes happen to our bodies as the aging process occurs. These deviations can be physical as well as mental. I am not certain, but there is an unmistakable change in your father's intellectual and psychological composition. This was evident during the examination. The problem is I am not sure what is the actual cause."

"Do you have any ideas?" asked Beth.

"I think I do, but before I even speculate, I would like to see the results of the current lab work. Also I think your father should see Dr. Spigai."

"Who is Dr. Spigai?" inquired Kathleen.

"She is relatively new to our area and quite competent in geriatrics, the diseases and care of the elderly."

"What about you? After all, you have been our family's doctor for years," said Kathleen.

"I just want her to examine your father. I will remain his primary physician."

"Could you just tell us if there is anything serious?" pleaded Kathleen.

"Again, I prefer to wait for the test results, but as far as I have observed, there appears to be nothing life-threatening or critically pressing at this point."

He shook each of their hands. "Schedule another appointment with me after your father has seen Dr. Spigai. By then, we will have a pretty good idea of what we are dealing with."

They rejoined their father and, for the first time, saw a little, gray-haired man sitting in the waiting room. Mrs. Berger arranged for the geriatric specialist to see Fred after Thanksgiving. After paying the bill, the three protectively surrounded their father and led him to the car.

T E N

The festivity of the holiday masked the week's previous events. Deborah and Donald drove in on Wednesday. With Mary Anne and her family, they stayed at Fred's house. With his children and grandchildren filling a void, Fred returned to his old self. Merriment and enthusiasm prevailed as the preparations were finalized. During this time, Fred sat with his grandchildren or the men, and watched contentedly as his daughters scurried about the kitchen and dining room.

Both Mary Anne and Deborah were updated by their sisters about their father's status. Both were stunned by the news. He had been their anchor for years and any compromise in his health uprooted the entire family. Every person in the house owed a great deal to Fred. His perpetual unselfishness and personal sacrifices were known by each member and deeply appreciated.

While the men were outside in the yard, Deborah spoke to her sisters, "I was going through a few items on the kitchen table and discovered these." She held up some papers.

"What are they?" asked Vera.

"They are bills and final notices from various companies,

including the utility company. Daddy has not paid his bills and they are threatening to cut off service."

"How could that be?" inquired Mary Anne. "He certainly has enough money."

"That's what we all assumed, but is it so?" questioned Vera.

Deborah added, "Does anyone here really know the extent of Daddy's assets and total income?" Each responded negatively. "It seems to me we'd better get to the bottom of this, fast. Tomorrow, let's sit down and discuss this with him." Thinking for a moment, she then suggested, "Let me broach the subject and then we can see what is actually happening."

The next morning during breakfast, Deborah tactfully brought up personal finances. With everyone in attendance, Fred found his checkbook and other important papers that had arrived recently. Deborah sifted through the mail and statements. "Donald, why don't you and Daddy go into town for a few hours. Get him a haircut and pick up a few items for the house." Her husband knew instinctively something was wrong and followed her directions without question. Once they had left, Deborah turned to her sisters and said, "We have a serious problem!"

"What is it?" queried Beth.

"Things are even worse than I anticipated. Not only has Daddy not been paying bills but he also has not deposited his last several pension and government checks." Frustrated, she continued, "The checkbook is a mess and it will take hours just to straighten it out and then pay the bills...." She held her hands to her face and sobbed silently.

Kathleen embraced her sister. With tears in her eyes, she said, "We are a family and we are going to have to find a solution. No matter how painful, it has to be fixed."

Deborah wiped her eyes. "I can work on the checkbook and bills. Can anyone go to the bank and make these deposits?"

"What about Daddy's endorsements?" asked Mary Anne.

"You're right, let me call the bank and speak to Mr. Meisel,"

Deborah said. She spoke at great length to the bank president. After hanging up, she added a few more instructions. "Mr. Meisel will give you some papers, please bring them to me."

"What are they?" inquired Vera.

"They are legal documents I will require: power of attorney and other things. Mr. Meisel knows what needs to be done."

Vera and Beth left, leaving the three other sisters to reconcile their father's financial affairs. Deborah spent several hours on the telephone, explaining to creditors the circumstances and assuring each that payment was forthcoming. By the time Fred and Donald came back, Deborah and her sisters had most of the paperwork done.

"Daddy, I would like to have you sign some papers for me."

"What for?"

Trying not to alarm or upset her father, Deborah answered. "These are documents that will enable all of us to sign your checks. I have spoken to Mr. Meisel and he suggested that it be done this way. Since you cannot get to the bank easily, Kathleen can now do your deposits."

Fred agreed and signed in the appropriate spaces. More relaxed, the five daughters embraced their father. Vera gave him a big kiss on his cheek and returned to her chair.

"Daddy, I was just wondering, where is your will?" asked Deborah.

"I am not sure."

"Is it in the house or at the lawyer's office?"

"I don't remember."

Deborah called Mr. Lane, her parents' attorney. "It appears neither you nor Mother ever filled out the necessary documents. There is no will!" Fred did not answer and instead picked up David and bounced him gently on his lap. "I will prepare the proper papers tonight," Deborah said quietly.

While cooking the leftover turkey, Kathleen pulled Deborah aside. "Do you think we have moved too fast with Daddy? After all, he hasn't even seen Dr. Spigai as yet!"

"Kath, you saw the hodgepodge we just had to correct. If we allow Daddy to continue like this, there is no way he will be capable of handling these affairs. It is up to us, as his daughters, to perform these functions. There is no choice." Hugging her sister tenderly, she went on, "Don't you think it hurts me inside. This is my father, not a stranger. The pain I feel is as strong as any of you feel, if not more. I am loaded with guilt, but there is no alternative. Daddy is no longer competent in these areas."

"I suppose you are right, but..."

"I know." After wiping the tears from one another's eyes, they helped their other sisters serve dinner.

Deborah carefully drew up a formal last will and testament. With everyone sitting at the table, she slowly read and explained every detail of its contents. Though simple, it was complete and covered every phase of Fred's financial and personal worth. Everyone, except for Fred, fully understood its ramifications. Fred sat quietly and listened to the proceedings. He did not ask a single question or demand a change; instead, he obediently signed when requested. Mr. and Mrs. Marone, their long-time neighbors, served as witnesses.

Deborah tried to stay strong, but despite all her training and legal experience, she felt the distress and misery along with all her sisters. She cried herself to sleep in Donald's arms later that night. He attempted to console his wife, but inwardly, he felt his own pain; it brought back personal memories he had deliberately suppressed.

ELEVEN

The next day, while the family took Fred shopping, Deborah remained at the house and finalized all the paperwork. When they returned, she took them into the dining room, and interpreted every detail. As she had done in the past, Deborah asked each sister along with their father to sign the documents. Upon completion, she looked up, "We are done now, Daddy, there is nothing more to worry about."

Fred was not sure how to respond; he thanked her and then turned to each of his children. "I love each of you very much and I hope I have not been too much of a problem for any of you." He slouched forward and added, "To grow old is one thing, but to become this way is another."

Vera hugged her father tightly and the others moved to his side. "We will not let you down, Daddy, all of us will be here if you need us."

On Sunday, each daughter left for her own home. Fred stood at his door and waved goodbye. As the last left, he closed the door and headed to the kitchen. Everything was neat and in place. Opening the refrigerator, he removed the remains of the Thanksgiving turkey and ate a few pieces. He then went to his bedroom. All night, the turkey sat on the kitchen table and the door to the refrigerator remained open.

T W E L V E

K athleen arrived early the next morning. She stared with enormous sadness at the spoiled food and open door. Quietly, she threw out the spoilage and tidied the area. Moving to her father's bedroom, she knocked at the door. Hearing no reply, she peeked inside.

She stared at the huddled form sleeping soundly in the bed. With mixed emotions, she nudged him gently. Fred became startled, but after recognizing Kathleen, he smiled. She said, "Come on, lazybones, we have to take you to see the doctor."

"I'm sorry, I guess I overslept. I'll be ready in a few minutes."

"Don't rush, we still have some time."

She waited in the kitchen until he arrived. With daughterly instincts, she rearranged his shirt and straightened his tie. After kissing him on the cheek, she quipped, "And now, handsome, we are going to see Dr. Spigai."

THIRTEEN

The drive ended in front of the University Hospital. After parking, they walked to the front entrance. Fred clung tightly onto Kathleen's arm as the elevator stopped on the eleventh floor. Exiting, they walked until reaching Suite 1105. She gave him a tender kiss on his cheek before entering the office.

The receptionist cheerfully took their information and ushered them into the doctor's office. Father and daughter waited. Within minutes, a youthful woman walked through the door and introduced herself.

"Good morning, my name is Dr. Lorraine Spigai. You must be Fred Lorins." She extended her hand and greeted him warmly. Turning to Kathleen, she asked her relationship and purpose for coming. Rather than taking notes, she discreetly turned on a small recording device. Her friendly approach charmed Fred. The hour passed swiftly and during that time, Dr. Spigai formulated a tentative diagnosis.

"I would like to run some tests on you, Fred. They are basically painless, but should give us a truer indication of what is actually going on in your body. Unless either of you has any objections, we can start today."

Fred did not say a word, but looked for approval from his daughter. "How long will the test be?" Kathleen queried.

"Today, we will merely draw some blood and take a urine sample. On the next visit, I will have some psychological and physical tests performed. Once these are completed and the results obtained, then we can meet again to discuss them."

Dr. Spigai drew the blood samples herself. While Fred walked to the examination room to collect a urine specimen, Kathleen spoke openly to the doctor. She expressed her family's concern and their desire to do everything possible to help their father, regardless of the cost.

"I understand your sincerity and can only assure you I will do the very best I can for your father. I treat all my patients as if they were my own father or mother. The specialty of geriatrics is relatively new to medicine and, I might add, quite difficult to handle from a professional point of view. Innately, we each deny the aging process and never fully comprehend its ramifications until it is too late." She compassionately touched Kathleen's hand, "I only hope I can help in some way, but all this is academic. We must await the results of the testing."

Their conversation was interrupted by Fred's entrance. Both said goodbye to Dr. Spigai. In the car, they discussed the day's events and agreed that the young physician's humanistic approach was compatible with Fred's needs and desires.

FOURTEEN

Over the next week, the series of examinations were undertaken. To give herself time to properly evaluate the results, Dr. Spigai called Kathleen and postponed their next meeting. Meanwhile, Mary Anne designed large signs for their father's house. With each one strategically located, they acted as a visual reminder. The one on the refrigerator boldly read, "SHUT THE DOOR." Every message was simple and concise, and more importantly, it served its function admirably.

To relieve Kathleen of the entire burden, each daughter, with the exception of Deborah, took responsibility for calling their father on a prearranged day of the week to check on his status. Kathleen and Vera cooked many of their father's meals. On weekends, a schedule included everyone but Deborah. Periodically, she and Donald would fly in and stay for an extended visit to relieve the others. With the signs and close supervision, Fred functioned relatively safely. No one complained. They did what was expected, not out of duty, but out of compassion for their father.

On the day of the appointment with Dr. Spigai, every daughter insisted on attending. Meetings were canceled, previous engagements rescheduled, and every other responsibility became secondary. Their utmost concern was their father and his future.

Once introductions were completed, Dr. Spigai opened Fred's chart and started to speak, "I want to thank you all for coming and showing this admirable interest in your father's health. It is often very frustrating for me when no one else is at all concerned, other than the patient. Yours is the type of relationship every geriatric specialist hopes to find."

After pausing briefly, she continued, "All the results are in and I have called Dr. Kole. We discussed the 0findings and I made several suggestions to him regarding Fred's treatments." Dr. Spigai spoke directly to Fred, not permitting him to play a secondary role. He nodded and then looked to Kathleen to reinforce his assent.

It was Deborah who broke the ice. "Could you tell us more of your findings and their implications?"

"The tests showed Dr. Kole correctly diagnosed the asthma, rheumatoid arthritis, and diabetes. We have suggested several modifications in the medications and I feel he should be the one to discuss these changes with you. He is extremely competent, and I was impressed with his interest and knowledge. We also have determined that a slight change of diet is indicated and I have these recommendations here." She handed the papers to Kathleen, "Look at these when you get home and should there be any problems, just let me know."

"Is that all?" asked Vera.

"No, there is one other item we must be concerned with."

"What is it?" asked Mary Anne impatiently.

"Physically, Fred, you are status quo, as best as I can determine after speaking to Dr. Kole. Mentally and psychologically, however, there is a slight deviation. The tests reveal the same and I have spoken to several psychiatrists on staff to confirm the results. A deviation from the norm was noted by all of us."

"Could you please speak so we can all understand?" asked Kathleen.

"I'm sorry, we doctors have a way of doing that when we are attempting to skirt an issue. Fred, you are suffering from an organic disease of the brain. It is, I'm sorry to say, slowly progressive and, at this time, incurable."

Deborah inquired, "What is the prognosis?"

"We are not sure. There is simply not enough information available about the disease itself. It could go into remission at any time, or maintain a steady course. Only time will tell."

"What can we do?" questioned Vera.

"At this point, nothing. There is, however, some research being done by a colleague at the university. Perhaps you would like to speak to him directly?"

"How can we reach him?" asked Deborah.

"I will make the arrangements and have him contact one of you. By the way, I would like to see you again, Fred, so I have a means of comparison."

"Certainly," answered Beth for Fred and the others.

Dr. Spigai then described Fred's condition. She simplified the complex and reassured everyone their father could easily last for quite some time. By the time the session had ended, every daughter was still somewhat apprehensive over Fred's status. Everyone was pleased, however, with Dr. Spigai and the professional way she handled the situation. Fred himself appeared to understand some of the context, but chose to remain silent.

Their game plan was simple: Arrangements had to be made to see Dr. Kole and a return visit to Dr. Spigai. Until these occurred, the daughters would care for their father the best they could.

FIFTEEN

Within a week, Dr. Spigai had Fred screened for the research project. Dr. Shapiro was the physician in charge of the program. Unlike Drs. Kole and Spigai, Kevin Shapiro was all business; there was little patient-doctor relationship among the project's subjects and the researchers. Fred arrived for each visit, was tested, and then received a designated number of pills for the week.

None of the subjects had any idea as to the pill's name or purpose. Like sheep, each received their assigned amounts every session, and then returned the next week for further instructions. Fred's progression leveled off and he functioned somewhat better. Dr. Spigai acted as a link between the two physicians, Kole and Shapiro.

With an upturn in her father's condition, Kathleen was able to devote more time to her immediate family's needs. Her other sisters did what they could, but the rest remained restricted by time and distance. Fred spent his days watching television or speaking to Mrs. Keeley, his new housekeeper. Deborah had arranged and was personally financing the domestic help. Because of her schedule and inaccessibility, Deborah felt compelled to help her father and this seemed to be the only method she could devise.

Mrs. Keeley arrived early in the morning during the week. She prepared Fred's breakfast, made sure he took the proper dosage of medication, and did light housekeeping. After supper she would leave, making sure everything was in order. On weekends, the four sisters who lived locally cared for their father. The plan worked well and took all the pressure off the family members, especially Kathleen.

The holidays came and passed quickly. As usual, Fred's house was the center of activity. Deborah and Donald stayed for an entire week and treated Fred to a completely new wardrobe. It had been years since he had purchased anything for himself, and Deborah made up for lost time.

As February approached, the strategy was holding well. All three doctors were extremely pleased with Fred's progress and the patient himself seemed to appreciate, within his limited scope, his new lease on life.

S I X T E E N

O n the first Friday of March, an unexpected blizzard struck. Accumulations up to three feet paralyzed every roadway and vehicle for miles around. With many of the telephone lines downed by fierce winds and snowy conditions, communications were impossible. Because of the inclement weather, Mrs. Keeley could not keep her scheduled assignment on Friday. Kathleen and her sisters tried, but none could reach their father or each other because of the hazardous weather. All day Friday and for most of Saturday, the telephones were useless. When service was finally restored, all calls to Fred's house went unanswered. Fred's daughters were frantic, but with the roads still treacherous, not even the police could check on their father's status.

Harold was finally able to make it through with his four-wheel drive vehicle. He and Kathleen maneuvered along the snow-covered streets. Instead of parking in Fred's unplowed driveway, Harold drove the truck right up to the front porch. The couple wallowed their way up the stairs. Shoving the front door open, they burst inside and shouted for Fred. Hearing no response, they turned on the lights and separated to search the house.

Kathleen's piercing cry vibrated throughout rooms and hallways. Harold rushed to her side. The cellar door was open and at the bottom of the steps lay Fred. Harold held his wife as she struggled to gain control, then he swiftly descended the fifteen steps. His father-in-law was semiconscious and apparently injured. Fred winced in pain as Harold touched his left leg.

"Call for help!" he shouted to his wife. Kathleen stared paralyzed for several more seconds, before moving to the phone. It took an hour before the ambulance could arrive, but once there, the crew examined their patient and skillfully maneuvered Fred onto a stretcher. After lifting him up the stairs, they wrapped the stretcher snugly in blankets, and then cautiously placed Fred in the ambulance.

Harold and Kathleen followed the flashing red light to the hospital, where Kathleen called Vera to explain what had occurred. After hanging up, she returned to her husband's side and waited.

SEVENTEEN

Within a few minutes, a tall nurse approached the couple. "Are you Mr. Lorins' daughter?"

"Yes."

"Would you please come with me, the doctor wishes to speak to you."

Without waiting to be asked, Harold walked at her side into the emergency room. Fred was lying on his back, comfortable but in some distress. Upon seeing his daughter, he reached out and instantly shouted in pain.

The nurse urged him to be still and offered Kathleen a seat next to her father's bed. "Doctor Waxey will be right with you."

After the nurse had pulled the curtain, Kathleen leaned over to get a closer view of her father. Tenderly stroking his forehead, she reassured him he was now safe. Harold stood to the side and watched his stricken father-in-law with great concern.

The curtain was abruptly pushed aside, and a slender male physician moved toward the bed. A stethoscope hanging loosely from his neck, he extended a hand toward Harold. "I'm Doctor Waxey." Looking at Fred for a moment, he turned to Kathleen.

"Your father has seriously injured himself from the fall. I have taken the liberty to call Drs. Spigai and Kole. From them, I have obtained a good background of your father's medical history. Both concur with my proposed treatment."

"What exactly is wrong with my father?"

"The x-rays reveal a dislocated right shoulder and a fracture to the left femur. Both injuries must be cared for immediately. Other than those two items, he has multiple contusions and hematomas throughout his trunk and extremities. An electroencephalogram and electrocardiogram revealed results within his normal limits. Luckily, we had Dr. Shapiro's data on hand, otherwise we would have had no means of comparison."

"What is going to be done?"

"With your permission, I will reset his dislocation and then have him prepared for surgery on the leg."

"Surgery?"

"I'm afraid we have no choice. The site of the fracture will necessitate some sort of internal fixation." He explained in great detail the surgical approach he intended to use and made them aware of every possible problem. Kathleen signed the consent forms and watched helplessly as her father was wheeled down the tiled hallway and into the elevator.

Time passed ever so slowly for Harold and Kathleen as they waited for word of Fred's progress. They called Vera every hour and it was her responsibility to notify the others. Finally Dr. Waxey walked into the waiting room dressed in his green surgical gown. He pulled up a chair, "The surgery went well and your father is now in the recovery room." Looking at his watch, he continued, "He will probably be in there for another hour or so. Since the storm, the hospital has been operating on short staff. I'd rather have him there than in his room, he'll get more attention and closer observation."

"What are his chances?" asked Kathleen.

"It is hard to say precisely, but all of his vital signs are stable and both procedures went exactly as I expected. Orthopedically, the surgery was a success."

"How long will he have to say in the hospital?" inquired Harold.

"That is difficult to say for sure. I can only judge his orthopedic progress; but the final say should come from Dr. Spigai. She will be your father's attending physician during his stay at the hospital. Now if you don't mind, I'd like to excuse myself and try to get some sleep. I will speak to you later."

They thanked him for his help and watched as he left the room.

EIGHTEEN

The next few days were uncertain. Fred was medically stable and was soon moved to a private room. Harold returned to work, while Vera and Beth periodically relieved Kathleen. Though he reported soreness and discomfort, Fred rested.

Drs. Spigai and Shapiro controlled each pill Fred took, and under this close scrutiny, their patient became mentally alert. Every daughter telephoned each day and spoke at length with their father.

Dr. Waxey monitored Fred's orthopedic progress and finally ordered physical therapy. Advancement was slow being greatly limited by age and overall mental status. No matter how hard he tried, independent mobility remained a long way off. Despite constant urging by the staff and his family, Fred could not master the process.

Since Deborah's busy schedule did not permit her to fly home even for a short time, she maintained a steady dialogue with Vera. It was Kathleen, however, who spent the most time at the hospital and became the chief decision-maker for the group.

On the fourth day of hospitalization, Ms. Lett from the institution's social service department introduced herself to Kathleen.

"With the new government regulations affecting the hospital, we must begin to consider what you are going to do after he is discharged."

Shocked by the statement, Kathleen responded, "I don't understand, can't my father stay here until he is better?"

"Absolutely not, once he is medically stable, the hospital must ask him to leave or find a suitable place for him to go."

"What is he to do? He does have a broken leg and non-functioning arm."

"I am fully aware of your father's condition. We do not have a choice, he must leave when ready."

"What did Dr. Waxey or Dr. Spigai say?"

"Neither can say anything that will change the decision, those are the government regulations."

"What can we do with him? He can't stay at his home in this shape."

"Can he stay with you or any other relative?"

Hesitating for a moment, Kathleen responded, "I think it would be impossible for my father to live with me, even for a short time. My house is already too small for my family."

"Is there anyone else who would take him?"

Thinking of each of her sister's situations, she shook her head. "I don't really think any of them could have him stay at their homes or apartments. When do you need an answer by?"

"Probably within the next two days. I must warn you if the answer is no, then other plans must be made quickly."

"Such as what?"

"There are plenty of fine nursing homes in the area that can accommodate your father."

"A nursing home!" she cried. "My God, how can you put my father in that kind of place?"

"Please understand the final decision is not mine. It belongs to you and your family. I am here to assist you in finding a solution."

"Are there any other options for us?"

"He could always return home and have someone stay with him. Many people select that method."

"Who would stay with him?"

"Many agencies supply help, this choice is expensive unless the family does a great deal themselves."

Stammering slightly, "My God!" Kathleen said, "I must speak to my sisters. Please give me a little time."

"I can only give you, at the most, two or three days. At that point, the hospital will probably try to get him discharged. By the way, should you decide any method short of taking him to his home or to one of yours, the government will require certain proof of your father's personal and financial statements."

"Why?"

"To see if he qualifies for public assistance."

Kathleen could only shake her head in disbelief as the social worker left. Feeling helpless, she immediately called Vera and arranged for a family meeting at her house later that night.

NINETEEN

Everyone was able to attend except Deborah. She was briefed by phone and atypically, flew off the handle. "How can they do that to anyone!" she shouted. "My father has rights...." Kathleen explained what had transpired, but her sister ranted on. "I will speak to this Ms. Lett personally and straighten this mess out."

After hanging up, Kathleen summarized the conversation and told her sisters of Deborah's plan. Each relaxed somewhat until Vera raised the question, "What if Deborah is wrong?"

"Yes," asked Beth. "What do we do then?"

"Can he stay with any of us?" asked Vera.

No one spoke. It was finally Mary Anne who said, "How can any of us have Daddy in our homes? We either do not have the time or the space."

"But he is our father!" cried Kathleen. "He gave everything to us!"

"I know, but what are we to do? We all have other responsibilities. Are we to forsake them?" responded Beth.

"I don't know, but there must be something we can do?" pleaded Kathleen. "I cannot do this alone, I need your help."

"What about Daddy going home and all of us helping?" asked Vera.

"I had thought about that but I don't think it will work. Mrs. Keeley is not strong enough to help Daddy. He is in poor physical shape," stated Kathleen. "More importantly, the doors are too narrow for a wheelchair and the house is not suitable for a handicapped person."

"How are you so sure?" asked Beth. "I spoke to Daddy's physical and occupational therapists. They told me what to look for and how to determine his ability to get around in the house."

"What are we going to do?" sobbed Vera.

"If Deborah cannot straighten out Ms. Lett, then we will have no choice. Daddy will have to go for a short time to a nursing home," stated Mary Anne. "Remember it is only on a temporary basis. Once he is better, he can go home."

"Has anyone spoken to the doctors about this?" asked Vera.

"No, but I plan on calling Dr. Spigai after I hear from Deborah," said Kathleen.

They ended their conversation, each depressed over their father's future. None wanted Fred to be placed in a nursing facility, and yet, none could care for him.

TWENTY

Deborah spent a frustrating and unproductive day. After speaking to Ms. Lett and getting nowhere, she called the hospital's executive administrator. Though enormously sympathetic to her plight, he did not buckle to her numerous threats or appeals. Out of desperation, she telephoned the State Health Department's legal section and again found the new regulations were rigid and precisely written. There was no appeal process and her father's discharge was imminent.

Vera utilized every channel within her grasp. The visually impaired society could offer no advice, nor could any of her professional colleagues. Out of desperation, she solicited the help of her local congressman. He, like the others, explained the inadequacies of the present law, but could offer no assistance. Unless one of his daughters could care for him, Fred had no choice but to be admitted to a nursing home.

Kathleen met with her father's three primary physicians and, though all were sensitive to their patient's needs, they were impeded by the hospital's discharge policies. They could perhaps delay his release by a few days, but any long-term commitment was impossible.

Mary Anne contacted an old friend who was employed at the town's only newspaper. During lunch, she explained her family's dilemma and sought solutions. Thomas had known Fred for years, but realized immediately the older man's fate was probably sealed. He offered to publish an editorial based on the difficulties of the elderly, but even a condensed article would take weeks to cause any effect. Disheartened by the meeting, Mary Anne called several other neighboring dailies, but, as with Thomas' paper, no fast answer could be found.

Beth called the hospital and obtained a listing of the institution's board of directors. For the next eight hours, she visited or called every name on the roster. Everyone was interested in her predicament, but none had the power to override the rulings. Several called the hospital's executive to gain more information, but most politely listened and promised to bring the matter up at the next board meeting. Not a single person would commit themselves to help their father.

Later that night, the five sisters compared the results of the day's events. By the time the summary was finished, every daughter was distressed and fully cognizant of what lay ahead. They formulated their plan and prepared for the worst. The event each ultimately feared had arrived, and with a united effort, they had to decide their father's destiny.

T W E N T Y - O N E

The five Lorins formed a semicircle with Dr. Spigai. Each sister apprehensively stared at the door. A turning of the knob caused every eye to focus as the door slowly swung inward. An aide maneuvered Fred and his wheelchair into the center of the group and then left the room. Fred looked at each of his daughters and smiled.

It was Dr. Spigai who spoke first, "Fred, you are looking quite well today. I trust you are feeling better."

"Yes, I am," he answered, hesitating slightly. "I didn't expect this."

"I should have told you this morning during my rounds. Please accept my apologies, I guess I had so many other things on my mind, I simply forgot."

Fred nodded and then reached his hand outward to grasp Beth's hand. He looked to her face and observed she was crying. "What is wrong?" he asked in a fatherly tone. His daughter could not respond, but looked to Dr. Spigai for help.

"Fred, your daughters and I are here today to discuss your future."

"What do you mean, my future?"

"What you are going to do after the hospital discharges you."

He thought for a moment and then spoke, "What do you mean by that?"

"I mean where are you going to stay?"

"I have a home!"

"I know, but in your physical condition, how are you going to take care of yourself?"

Thinking momentarily, Fred continued, "Mrs. Keeley will be there to help me if needed. Otherwise, I can do the rest myself."

"How can you get around the house? The wheelchair will not fit through your doorways and you cannot walk yet."

"Mrs. Keeley is very strong; she can help me."

"I'm afraid Mrs. Keeley cannot help, we have spoken to her. She recently hurt her back and cannot do any lifting."

"Then my children will help." He looked around the room at his daughters for support.

"Your children can only assist to a point. Each has her own life to lead. None can devote her full-time energies to your care."

"Kathleen!" he cried out. "What is happening here?"

Dr. Spigai continued, "Fred, if you were to go home right now, the question is, how could you survive? You are thinking more logically than you have in quite some time and the reason is simple: The nurses at the hospital have been monitoring your medications. Who will do it for you at home?"

"I don't need anyone, I can do it myself!" Fred shouted defiantly.

"And what if you forget?"

"My daughters would help me. Kathleen, tell her!"

His eldest daughter gently touched his hand and then spoke softly, "She's right, Daddy."

"What do you mean she's right? I am your father and need your help. Why are none of you helping me? I was always there for you."

"Fred, do you remember falling?"

"No."

"That's what your daughters are afraid of. None wants you to get hurt again." Fred did not speak a word, but stared in disbelief at his five daughters. "I have suggested to your family that you be sent to a skilled nursing facility for further care."

"You mean an old age home?"

"Not exactly. We do not refer to these as old age homes any longer. They are wonderfully equipped and the nurses will monitor your medications daily."

Turning to his children, Fred spoke in a suddenly icy tone, "How can you do this to me?"

"Fred, this could be only a short-term situation. With additional physical therapy, your walking will improve. At that point, there is a chance you could go home," Dr. Spigai attempted to reason with Fred.

"A chance?"

"That will depend on you."

"Deborah, why are you letting them do this to me?" For the first time in her life, Deborah was at a loss for words.

As articulate as she had become, she could not make herself respond. "Daddy." was all she could say.

"Daddy? Is that all I get? Is this what I deserve from any of you? All my sacrifices for each of you and look at what I get in return! Your mother was luckier than me, she died."

"Fred, your children are only concerned with your welfare. That is why this must be done. It is what is best for you in the long run," Dr. Spigai explained calmly.

"How would you know what is best for me? I do not want to go to a nursing home. I want to live in my own house and I want to sleep in my own bed. I will take care of myself! I don't need any of you!"

Angrily glaring at each of his children, he uttered, "How could any of you do this to your own father?"

Realizing the conversation was not progressing, Dr. Spigai telephoned the nurses' station. Within minutes, an aide wheeled Fred back to his room. He did not speak another word to anyone, but only glowered one by one at each of his children.

After he left the room, all the women broke down in tears. Dr. Spigai tried to comfort them as best she could; however her words of encouragement did no good. They returned to their homes and lives.

TWENTY-TWO

Two days later, Fred was discharged from the hospital and placed in the Southeastern Nursing Home. He refused to speak to any of his family. At the home, he spurned the staff. Dr. Spigai ordered several new medications in hopes of elevating his spirits, but a change never occurred. He did not eat and spit out his pills when no one was looking. The decline was rapid and within a few short weeks, Fred Lorins died.

Reunion

O N E

Nathan and Marsha Edwards lived comfortably in an unpretentious Cape Cod house in Yorktown. Retired for the past three years, Nathan spent most of his time looking for ways to keep himself occupied. He had worked since high school, and the transition from an active to a sedentary role was difficult. During the warmer weather, he busied himself with outdoor pursuits; however the winter greatly restricted his activities. During inclement conditions, watching television and reading his mail were Nathan's primary entertainment.

Marsha, on the other hand, was remarkably energetic and engrossed in her many hobbies and interests. From early morning to bedtime, she veered from one activity to the next. Her dynamism was plentiful and amazed everyone, including all her seven children. Nathan accepted his wife's tremendous enthusiasm and had learned to live with her idiosyncrasies over the past fifty-five years. Having spent most of her life caring for her children's needs, she welcomed her newfound independence with zeal. Though she tended to her husband's needs, Marsha's primary goal was literally to make up for lost time.

Nathan by nature functioned with exactness. Days were usually just the same as the previous one. He rose every morning at 6:30 a.m. After showering, he made himself breakfast. Once the dishes were cleaned, he sat in his oversized easy chair and turned on the television. Regardless of the weather, he remained there until 10 a.m. During this time, he would become absorbed in the morning news and several talk shows. He never deviated, always watched the exact same programs each morning.

At the end of the Frank Marcus Show, he would walk to the front window and keep an eye out for Mr. Roye. The mail carrier usually brought the mail by 10:15 a.m. Even in the worst of weather, delivery was within a twenty-minute range. Nathan waited until the morning's mail was actually in the box. After Mr. Roye had descended the porch, Nathan would scurry out the front door and retrieve whatever was brought. He carefully read every piece of mail addressed to his name, their names, or anything titled "occupant." Only Marsha's mail was left unopened.

After some housekeeping chores, Marsha would immediately organize her daily activities. She generally ate a fast breakfast and then dressed. Ignoring the television, she would scan the mail. Her planned endeavors filled the remainder of the day and evening. Nathan often watched his wife scurry about or found some mundane activity to occupy his time.

On weekends, their children periodically stopped by to visit. This would drastically interrupt Nathan's routine. He enjoyed his grandchildren and played endlessly with every one. Occasionally, he and Marsha would drive over to their sons' or daughters' homes, but this was exceedingly rare as Nathan resisted using their automobile. The high price of gasoline and their limited budget reinforced his negative attitude toward driving. Rather than argue, Marsha accepted her husband's decision, and had to forego any thoughts of taking an extended vacation.

Weekly card games kept Marsha busy two afternoons a week. When the games were at their home, Nathan would casually observe. He spoke freely with her friends, but tended to remain passive most of the time. When his wife was away from the house, he watched television.

Both Dr. Glass, their family physician, and Marsha urged Nathan to increase his physical activities and to control his weight. Despite their pleas, he did not heed their recommendations. Though not exceedingly obese, he sported a large waistline and had difficulty maneuvering around the house.

Marsha maintained a petite figure and had kept her weight about the same since her wedding. Her blood pressure was slightly elevated, but Dr. Glass controlled it with medications. Her physician urged her to slow down slightly, but her intrinsic drive pushed her ahead.

T W O

The excitement of the holidays passed quickly. The severity of winter forced Marsha's activities to decline. Several of her card games were canceled due to poor weather conditions and the children's visits also reduced. For the most part, Nathan's life remained unchanged. With television and mail to connect him to the outside world, blizzards did little to stifle his activities.

One morning in mid-February, Nathan arose and followed his normal routine. As the clock chimed ten times, he strolled to the window and patiently waited for Mr. Roye. Time passed and still the mail hadn't arrived. Donning his outerwear and boots, he left the house. Nowhere could the mail carrier be seen. He walked through the snow-filled walkways until he spied a blue-gray uniform ahead. He picked up his pace until he confronted the carrier.

"Is everything okay, Mr. Roye?"

"Certainly! What brings you here, Mr. Edwards?"

"I was concerned. You are usually at our home by 10 a.m., and since you were late, I was just worried."

"That's very nice of you, but I got a late start this morning. The mail was held up at our central office because of the weather."

"Oh, I see."

"As long as you are here, do you want your mail?"

Not wanting to appear too eager, Nathan coolly responded. "I might as well, as long as I'm here. It will save you some time."

Mr. Roye located the Edwards' mail and then watched as the elderly man trudged back to his house. After removing his coat and boots, Fred was greeted by Marsha.

"Where have you been?"

"I went for the mail."

"Doesn't it usually get delivered?"

Instead of going into a long dissertation, Nathan walked to the dining room table and began sorting the letters. He stopped halfway through at a small envelope. Curious, he examined the return address.

"What's so interesting?" asked Marsha.

"It appears to be a letter from my old high school."

"Your high school?"

"Yes, can you imagine that…probably want money."

"Well, there is only one way to find out," she said. "Open it!"

He carefully ripped the envelope and withdrew the contents. Nathan silently read the message then smiled.

"Well, what is it? Come on, don't keep me in suspense. Did they ask for money?"

"No, I have just been invited to my sixty-year high school reunion."

"A high school reunion?"

Looking at the letter, he grinned. "Sixty-year reunion. Can you believe that? Sixty years already."

"When is it?"

Nathan reread the note. "It's being held in June. Up in Katyville."

"Katyville, I thought the place would have been plowed under by now."

He did not respond. It had been over fifty-nine years since he had seen Katyville. He wondered what it was like.

"Do you want to go?" asked Marsha.

"Where? To the reunion?" he replied.

"Where else?"

"It's a long way and besides, how many of my classmates could still be around?"

"You are! Maybe a few more of you have lasted."

"I don't think so," he softly said. "It is too far to travel."

Marsha did not respond to his answer; instead she picked up her knitting. He examined the rest of the mail and then rose from the table. For some reason, he did not throw away the invitation but rather placed it in the top drawer of his desk. Instead of discussing the topic any further, he turned on the television and watched his customary shows.

For the next few days Nathan attempted to maintain his usual routine. However, with their children and grandchildren paying a surprise visit, too much excitement was generated.

On the following Monday, Nathan retrieved his mail from the box and reentered the house. After looking over what had arrived that day, he remembered the invitation. While Marsha was in the kitchen, he slipped into the den and opened the top drawer. Reaching inside, he removed the letter. After rereading it once more, he grinned broadly as his mind raced across the many years .

"Nathan, where are you?"

Startled, he said, "I'm in the den. I'll be right there." He shoved the letter into the drawer and left for the kitchen.

"What were you doing in there?" asked his wife.

"Nothing. I was just looking for some papers," replied Nathan.

T H R E E

L eslie, their youngest daughter, invited Marsha to go shopping for the afternoon. Her mother accepted and dressed for the occasion. Nathan watched as she waited to be picked up. "You don't mind, do you?" asked Marsha.

"No, not at all."

"Do you want to come?"

"No, I have something to do around the house."

"Around the house? What are you talking about?"

"There is a show I want to see."

"That's what I thought." Hearing a honking outside, she kissed him lightly on the cheek and went outside to join her daughter.

"Have a good time, but don't spend too much money!" he called after her, but she did not answer.

Watching the car drive off, he walked straight to his desk and once again removed the invitation. He read the words carefully. "I wonder," he said softly. "I wonder…"

He placed the paper on the top of the desk and then went downstairs to the basement. He thought for a few moments and then strode to the far corner. Boxes filled the entire section and he

117

shook his head in disbelief. "Where do I start?" he said aloud as he tried to recall where the object of his quest might be located. Pulling up an old chair, he grabbed the nearest box. Gently opening the container, he discovered many of his son-in-law Jimmy's personal belongings. After searching the box, he repacked the contents and moved to another.

Nathan labored methodically at his task. He had inspected seven boxes when Marsha called from the top of the stairs. "Nathan, are you down there?"

"Yes," he shouted. "I was just looking for something. I'll be right up." He replaced everything and walked up the stairs. "Did you have a good time with Leslie?"

"Excellent. I did buy several things," Sharon announced.

Normally he would have delved into the subject of frugality but for some reason, he elected to let the matter slip by without any comment. Surprised, Marsha asked, "Are you okay?"

"Yes, why do you ask?"

"Oh, no reason. I was just wondering, that's all. By the way, how was the show?"

"What show?"

"The one you wanted to see today?"

"It was good," he hesitated. "Very good."

"What were you looking for in the basement?"

"Nothing important, I was just looking for something I lost." Determined to change the topic, he asked, "How are the kids doing?"

"Much better. Jeremy is still very hoarse, but the doctor says everything will be fine."

"Good," he said as he turned on the television. Marsha started supper and the couple ate a quiet meal. Nathan retired early that night while Marsha completed a few more rows of the sweater she was knitting. Before going to bed, she checked to make certain all the windows and doors were locked. As she wandered into the den, a piece of paper sitting on the desktop attracted her attention. She picked it up and read the note. Replacing it, she turned off the lights and joined her husband.

In the days that followed, Nathan slipped down to the cellar every chance he could and continued his search. It had been weeks, and still he had yet to uncover it. Marsha frequently questioned him as to his investigation, but he always answered vaguely. He had found many missing or misplaced objects, most of which belonged to his children. Clothes, books, and past mementos constituted the majority of items.

It was well into the fourth week when he found the book. Though dusty and discolored, it was in rather sturdy shape. After resealing the box, he went back to the den and placed it in the top drawer of the desk. Smiling, he joined Marsha. The next time he was alone, he would have plenty of time to explore the book's contents.

F O U R

The next day, Marsha left to visit an ailing friend. As soon as she departed Nathan retrieved both the invitation and the book. Settling back in his easy chair, he read the letter and placed it aside. Looking at the book's cover, he gazed at the raised letters: *Katyville High School Yearbook.*

Slowly turning the pages, he leafed through the many pictures and read most of the words that filled the pages. He came to his own picture. He looked at the youthful face and read the brief inscription beneath the photo. *Best remembered for his outgoing personality and athletic abilities. Activities: football, basketball, baseball, and track teams. Plans on entering the world of business after graduation.*

He reread the words several more times and then closed the book. *So many years,* he said to himself. *Where did the time go?*

He studied the book for another hour and then hid it, along with the invitation, in his desk. When Marsha returned, she discovered her husband in his usual position. Without trying to compete with the television, she entered the kitchen and prepared their supper.

That night as they lay in bed, Nathan turned on his side and spoke to Marsha. "I would like to ask you a question."

"Yes, what is it?"

"How would you feel about going to my reunion?"

"What reunion?"

"The one I received the invitation to. My high school reunion."

"That was a while ago. I thought you threw it away. When is it?"

"In a few months."

"Well, I have no objections to going, but can we afford it?"

He did not answer immediately. "I will call one of these days and speak to someone up there. I'll get an idea of prices since they were not listed on the invitation."

"Do you want to go?"

Without appearing too eager, he said, "I think we could use a vacation and the area is still nice, so I've been told. Maybe we can do both at the same time."

"Well, let me know what you want to do."

"I will." He kissed her on the cheek and then retired for the night.

FIVE

Nathan was up early and nervously found things to keep himself busy. For some reason, he could not tolerate his usual programs, and instead had to find other activities. Slowly the hands of the clock crept around its face. Finally at 10 a.m., he dialed the number printed on the invitation.

After a few rings, a party picked up the phone. "Good morning, this is Katyville Central School District. How can I help you?"

Bumbling for a few seconds, he spoke, "I would like to find out more about the reunion."

"Which reunion? There are many planned," the voice informed him.

"I received an invitation a while ago and would like to talk to someone about it. It is my sixty-year reunion."

"Oh, let me connect you to Arlene Welson. She is organizing the affair. Perhaps she can answer your questions. Please hold on and I'll get her."

A minute later, another voice spoke, "This is Arlene Welson, how can I help you?"

"I would like to get some information about my sixty-year

reunion. I received an invitation and—"

"Have you returned it?"

"No, not yet. I have some questions to ask."

"Certainly. But first, could you tell me your name?"

"Nat Edwards."

"Let me see. Yes, here it is. Nathan Lewis Edwards."

"Could you tell me if any others are coming?"

"We have sent out invitations to as many as we could locate. So far, we have had three positive responses. I am afraid I do not have those names right here."

"Do you remember any of them who are coming?"

"I'm sorry, it's just that we are having several different reunions within a two-month period. I simply cannot remember all the names," Ms. Welson explained.

"I understand. It's just that I was curious about certain people. It's been many years."

"Yours is the oldest reunion. Can I assume you will be coming?"

"I think so, but can I get more information about places to stay?"

"I will have a list sent to you. I do hope you will come. I am sure you would love to see your friends."

"I'm pretty sure my wife and I will attend. I'd like to plan our vacation at the same time."

"I will have the information sent out to you immediately."

"I'll return my card after I get the material." He hung up the receiver. After looking at the invitation one last time, he left it on the table and waited to tell Marsha the news.

S I X

Despite the weather, Nathan met Mr. Roye at the far corner of the block. Impatiently he scanned the mail in search of the reunion material. Finally after ten days of waiting, a large brown package arrived.

Arlene Welson had included the promised literature and more. Nathan studied the various maps and travel guides. Many more highways and motels filled the region than when he grew up. He was pleased to discover several within their limited budget.

When Marsha entered the room, he gave her a gentle hug. "My goodness, what is this all about?" she asked.

"Come here and see what came today."

He led her over to the material and watched her reactions as she sorted through the literature. "It looks interesting, but have you decided we're going?"

"Well, I'd like to, but the final decision is yours."

Smiling, she responded, "Yes, I think it would be nice. After all, I never really did see your hometown."

He kissed her on the cheek. "I will return the reply tomorrow. By the way, do you have any objections to staying at the Holiday

Motel? The reunion is being held nearby and they have a special price if we stay there."

Examining the brochure Marsha replied, "It seems like a nice place." Joking, she added, "As long as the sheets are clean and we don't have to share a bathroom with anyone else."

"I'll call after lunch and make a reservation."

As they ate Marsha noticed a definite change in her husband. The television had not been turned on yet and he was preoccupied with the reunion. While she washed the dishes, he made reservations with the motel.

"It's all set. The room is ours for four days."

"Four days?"

"Yes, I thought we'd stay a little longer to see the sights."

She smiled then walked to the dining room to begin her day's activities. Nathan followed her and sat at the table. "Aren't you going to watch television?" she asked.

"No, not now. I think I'll just look over my yearbook."

For the remainder of the morning, Nathan poured over the book and recalled details of his past.

S E V E N

Early the next morning, Nathan personally gave Mr. Roye his reunion response and urged him not to lose it. He left the newly arrived mail unopened on the dining room table and went to the den. Picking up the reunion literature, he impulsively dialed the phone.

"Can I speak to Mrs. Welson please?" After several moments, a voice answered. "Mrs. Welson, is that you?"

"Yes, who is this?"

"This is Nathan Edwards. I just want to tell you my wife and I will be attending my reunion. I sent in the response, but I wanted to tell you personally in case the mail gets lost."

"That was for the sixty-year reunion?"

"Yes, and by the way, has anyone else mentioned they are coming?"

"Yes, as a matter of fact, a Mr. George Baudes called yesterday to let us know he is also coming."

"You mean George is going to be there?"

"Yes, he's coming."

"Did he give you an address and phone number?"

"Yes."

"May I have it? I'd like to give him a call."

Mrs. Welson looked up the information and gave it to Nathan. He thanked her. Looking at the slip of paper, he smiled, *George, that son-of-a-gun. After all these years.*

Nathan did not tell Marsha about the call and patiently waited until she left the house. Carefully dialing, he waited while it rang.

"Hello."

"I was wondering if I could speak to a Mr. George Baudes?"

"Yes, one moment please." In the background, he heard a child scream, "Grandpa, it's for you!"

A minute later, an elderly sounding voice asked, "This is George Baudes, who is this?"

"George, this is Nat Edwards."

"Nat Edwards? I'm afraid you must have the wrong number."

"No, George, this is Nat Edwards who graduated with you from Katyville High School."

He thought for a while and responded, "Nat Edwards…my God! Nat Edwards!"

"Yes, I just got your name from a Mrs. Welson, who is organizing the reunion. She gave me your number."

"I see."

"I just wanted to call and say hello."

"This certainly is a surprise! It's been such a long time. Where do we begin?"

"I am not sure myself, but I'm glad to hear you will be going to the reunion. Will your wife be coming?"

"My wife died several years ago and I live by myself. Today, my grandchild is visiting. He's the one who answered the phone," explained George.

Not wishing to distress his longtime friend, Nathan changed his line of questioning. "I'm sorry about your wife. What did you do for a living, all these years?"

"Many different things, but I retired two years ago from the

Fuller Box Company. I was a supervisor."

"I retired a few years ago, and I find it absolutely terrible. I'm bored all the time!" Nathan confessed.

"Me too! All I do is watch television."

Nathan laughed, "That is all I do also. Do you think it has anything to do with our past?"

"No, I really don't think so."

"Have you kept in touch with anyone else?"

"No, you are the first I have heard from in quite some time. Do you remember Ralph Brown?"

"Yes, the football player."

"That's the one! Anyhow, he just died. I read it in one of the city papers."

"He's dead? He was in such good shape."

"That was many years ago, and we all have changed," reminded George.

"Not me," quipped Nathan. "I'm the same as I was when I graduated from high school. I'm just a little fatter, balder, and grayer."

"Is that all? I guess we are all about the same in those categories."

"How many children do you have?"

"A bunch and thank goodness I have all of them. Otherwise, I'd have no one."

"Except for my wife, my kids and grandchildren are all I have too," said Nathan.

"Who said getting old is golden?"

"Whoever said it, must have died young," Nathan replied.

They laughed and went on to several other topics. Suddenly, the conversation was interrupted by George's grandchild calling for help. "Nat, I have to go. My grandson needs some help. I'll see you at the reunion and thanks for calling."

Before Nathan could respond, he heard a click at the other end. He hung up the phone and stared at George's picture in the yearbook. Smiling, he reminisced about their previous escapades. "I can't wait for the reunion," he uttered. "I wonder who else will be there?"

EIGHT

Right after breakfast, Nathan descended the stairs to the basement. Marsha did not ask, but instinctively knew the venture had something to do with the reunion. He began searching the unopened boxes for yet another item. It took several more days before he found his sweater. Though wrinkled and a little mildewed, it still proudly displayed a large white "K" on a blue background. Holding it closer, he inspected the wool for moth holes. Finding none, he walked upstairs to show Marsha.

"Look what I found."

"Where did you find that old thing? I never saw it before!" she said.

"It was my high school sweater." Handing it to Marsha, he smiled as she examined the aged wool.

"It looks as if it is still in good shape. Try it on."

He carefully donned the sweater and moved to the mirror for a closer look. His smile quickly faded. The excess weight he had gained made the sweater ridiculously undersized. None of the buttons could be fastened as his enlarged belly pushed the edges far apart.

"At least the shoulders fit," consoled Marsha cautiously.

Nathan did not respond but became repulsed by what he saw. He vainly sucked in his stomach, but the edges still could not touch.

Marsha sensed his distress and moved to his side. "We all change Nat. The sweater looks terrific on my already handsome husband."

He continued to examine himself in the mirror. Finally, he said, "I am going on a diet. I will fit into this sweater by my reunion!"

"Why don't we see Dr. Glass first; I'm sure he could help," suggested Marsha.

"I don't need Dr. Glass; I can do it myself. Mark my words! I will fit into this sweater for my reunion."

She watched as her husband continued scrutinizing himself in the ill-fitted garment. After a prolonged silence, she added, "I will take it to the cleaners tomorrow after I go food shopping."

"I will go with you. I want to talk to them about it."

Nathan patiently waited for Marsha to return from an errand the next morning; instead of watching television, he looked at his yearbook, the sweater, and the reunion literature. When Marsha came in the door, Nathan blurted, "Why don't we go to the cleaners right now, and we can have brunch out."

"But—"

"No buts, let's just get going."

"Did my letter from Janie come yet?"

"I don't know. I forgot to look for the mail, but we can look at it later. I'm sure it will still be here when we get back."

He practically pushed her out the door and drove to the cleaners. He instructed the owner to exercise great care in cleaning the sweater and asked him to reinforce each button. They ate breakfast at a local restaurant and Marsha watched as her husband ate only low-calorie, nutritious foods. From there, they traveled to the supermarket and shopped for their weekly supplies. For the first time in years, Nathan did not select any snack food. Instead, he bypassed the aisle and went to the checkout.

After helping her unpack back in the kitchen, he sat in his chair and studied his material.

"Did you get the mail?" Marsha shouted from the kitchen.

"I forgot, why don't you get it?"

Now convinced a change had come over Nathan, she retrieved the day's mail. What belonged to Nathan, she left on the dining room table.

NINE

"Mom, is something wrong with Daddy?" inquired Marge.

"No, why do you ask?"

"Well, he is losing so much weight and is acting so different," she said.

"He's been on a diet and has already lost thirty pounds. He's doing it for his reunion."

"What reunion?"

"I guess I forgot to tell you. We are going to his high school reunion." She proceeded to tell her daughter of the details.

"Is that the reason for the change in his personality?"

"I assume so, he's like a new person. He rarely watches television and shows no interest in the mail. Instead, he takes regular walks and is getting himself into shape."

"Why?"

"God only knows, but I won't argue. I love the new man! I finally have an energetic companion."

Nathan was playing cards with Jimmy, his son-in-law, when the two women walked into the room.

"Daddy, why don't you tell Jim about your reunion?" asked

Nathan's daughter.

"What is there to tell? Your mother and I are going upstate to attend my high school reunion. We plan to stay a few extra days and sightsee."

"A reunion?" asked Jim. "How many years is it?"

"Five hundred," jested Nathan. "I graduated from the oldest class in the country."

"Really?" asked Michael, their grandson.

"Grandpa is just pulling your leg. Tell us the truth."

Picking up his grandson, Nathan kissed him on the cheek. "The truth is I graduated only one hundred years ago." Everyone laughed and proceeded to quiz Nathan. He answered their questions and then stood and walked into the den. He returned with his yearbook in hand. Turning the pages, he stopped and displayed a picture for all to see. "Can anyone guess who that handsome fellow is?"

His daughter peered at the picture. "Oh, Daddy, check out how young you look. You were so handsome."

"What do you mean 'were'?" teased Nathan.

"Oh! You still are!" she answered, embarrassed.

They read the inscription and then each took a turn skimming through the book. Everyone commented on the numerous pictures; Michael was most impressed with Nathan's football pictures.

"Grandpa, were you a star?"

"You might say that. I did quite well with the ball."

"Did you ever score a touchdown?"

"A few."

"Wow!" was all Michael could say. He gazed at the picture and then stared at his grandfather. His hero was gaining respect at a swift rate. "Mommy, why didn't you tell me that about Grandpa?"

"I didn't know, that's why! He never told me anything about his school days," Marge explained.

Looking at his watch, Nathan remarked, "I think we should put down the book and eat. I'm sure everyone is hungry by now."

No one argued the point as he and Marsha left for the kitchen.

Jimmy turned to Marge, "Why didn't you tell me about your father?"

"I honestly didn't know. He was always secretive about his past. All of this is a surprise to me also."

After eating supper, the family returned to the living room. Michael continued to be awestruck by his grandfather and grinned broadly when the older man placed him gently on his knee to tell him football stories.

T E N

Time flew as the weather warmed and Nathan spent longer periods outside. His walks were increasing in length and Marsha often did not see him for hours. Between her hobbies and his latest self-rehabilitation, the two spent only evenings together. With only one more week to go before the reunion, Nathan was physically and mentally preparing himself for the occasion.

Having lost so much weight, none of his clothes fit. When he arrived home with several packages, Marsha quizzed him as to the contents.

"Just sit right here and I will be back in a minute," he replied.

Five minutes later he wore a perfectly tailored slacks and shirt outfit. With matching socks and shoes, the garments were completely color coordinated.

"Where..." began Marsha, stunned by the transformation.

"Wait one more minute, I'm not done yet."

Opening the last package, he withdrew his high school sweater. He pulled on the garment and easily closed every button. Smiling broadly, he asked. "Well, how do I look?"

Marsha was in shock. Nathan looked outstanding. She kissed

him on the cheek and studied her "new" husband.

"How many pounds did you actually lose?" she asked.

"I stopped counting, but I can tell you my waistline is the same size as when I graduated from high school. I wonder if anyone will recognize me?"

"I can't see why not. Other than being grayer, you look about the same as your yearbook picture."

He laughed. "The crow's feet and wrinkles don't count?"

"Incidental items. You look absolutely marvelous, Nathan," Marsha said earnestly.

"Oh, by the way, I made an appointment for the car next week. I want it to be checked out before the trip," Nathan informed her.

As the final days closed, Nathan continued to diligently watch his diet and regulate his every activity. He walked into town and received a haircut. Everything was fitting nicely into place.

The night before their departure, the couple sat at the dining room table. Maps were spread out as they determined the best route for the trip. Nathan wanted to stop off along the way to observe points of interest. Since Marsha had never seen any of the area, she agreed amicably to his itinerary. She was eager to explore her husband's past and visit his hometown.

It took hours before the task was completed. Using a flare pen, he drew their route on the map and then placed it alongside their small traveling bag. "I guess we are ready for tomorrow," he remarked.

"I think so, but remind me about the sandwiches and cooler," Marsha requested.

He watched as she walked to the bedroom. "You go to bed, I will be right there. I just want to check a few more things." After she left, he double-checked every window to make sure it was securely locked. Even though Marge would come every day, he still worried about their home while they were away. He picked up his yearbook and studied each page. "Tomorrow, I return to my roots," he uttered to himself.

E L E V E N

The alarm startled Marsha and Nathan from a sound sleep. Silently, both dressed and completed the remainder of their preparatory tasks. Marsha made the beds and rechecked the house while Nathan packed the car. They ate quickly and after calling Marge, locked the front door. Their car started instantly. He permitted it to warm up for a few minutes and then turned to his wife. "Are you ready?"

"Whenever you are," she said eagerly.

"Do you have the traveling bag and map?"

"Right here."

"Good, then let's go!"

With exhilaration he hadn't felt in years, Nathan backed out of the driveway and toward the parkway. The traffic was building as they eased their way across Bear Mountain Bridge. Neither spoke but watched as the morning sun flashed brilliantly across the cloudless sky. Within an hour, they were on an open road with few cars moving in their direction. Marsha rechecked their progress whenever an exit would appear, but both realized there was still a long way to go.

After awhile, Marsha turned on the radio and they listened as an unfamiliar disk jockey played a variety of country music. Unable to tune in another clear station, the couple were obligated to hear alien tones and melodies. Since neither felt like talking, the strange sounds filled the car. Marsha's only escape was to take a short nap.

Nathan was ecstatic, but he kept it to himself. As he watched the passing exits, the excitement intensified. With his wife sleeping, he observed the scenery that slowly unfolded before his eyes. Unfortunately, nothing seemed familiar and the imagery in his memory differed greatly from reality. Moving along the high-speed roadway, many town and city names revealed themselves. With each one, a distant reminiscence entered his mind. Decades of absence caused Nathan to wonder what lay ahead.

Several hours later, he eased their automobile into a service station. The change of acceleration awakened Marsha. Looking around she asked, "Is everything okay?"

"Yes, I just thought I'd like to stretch for a few minutes."

"Where are we?"

"Just below Albany."

"We're making good time. Are you hungry?"

They consumed the ample lunch from their cooler. After finishing, Nathan eased the car back onto the road and headed northward. With Marsha navigating, they easily changed highways where necessary. For the rest of the day, they traveled with no difficulty. Every so often, they would stop and relax, but for the most part, Nathan was eager to reach his destination. By the time they arrived at their thruway exit, the sun was disappearing below the horizon. After paying a toll, the couple drove another two hours before rolling into Katyville.

A huge "Welcome to Katyville" sign greeted them as Nathan steered the car along the main highway. Flashing neon lights and the business district reduced their speed and forced Nathan to pull into the first service station. He got directions to the motel and within a few more minutes, they pulled into its parking lot.

Nathan surveyed the area then walked inside. A young girl stood behind the desk. "May I help you?"

"Yes, we are here to register." The employee handed them the information sheet and upon its completion, handed Nathan the room key. "By the way, has anyone else registered for the reunion?" asked Nathan.

"Several others have arrived, and more are due tomorrow," she replied.

"Can you tell me some of the names?"

"Jones, Wittingham, Hanson, Jackson..."

"Is that Jackie Jackson?"

The young girl checked the file. "Yes, a Mr. and Mrs. Jack Jackson have registered. They are in room 615."

Nathan was becoming more elated. He thanked the desk clerk and unloaded their car. "Can you imagine that? Jackie Jackson!" he said to his wife, "Do you mind if I call him in the morning?"

"Not at all, but let's get some rest. It was a long trip."

He kissed her and turned off the light. "Jackie Jackson..." He closed his eyes and soon fell into a restful sleep.

TWELVE

The alarm woke the couple. Nathan picked up the phone and dialed the operator. "Room 615 please."

After three rings, a female voice answered, "Hello."

"Is a Jackie Jackson there?"

"May I ask who's speaking?"

"I'd like to surprise him. I graduated from school with him."

"One moment please."

A few seconds later, a resonating male voice spoke. "This is Jackie, who is this?"

"Is this the Jackie Jackson who lived on Elm Street and the one who played end on the varsity football team?"

"Why, yes, but who is this?"

"I am a voice from the past: This is Nathan Edwards."

After a slight hesitation, Jackie recalled his friend, "Nathan....Nathan Edwards. You lived down the block. That's right, oh my God! Nathan Edwards!"

They spoke for almost a half-hour before Jackie suggested they meet in the lobby. "Excellent, we'll have breakfast and maybe tour the old town."

Nathan dressed and waited patiently for Marsha. Together they walked to the motel's main lobby. Noticing no one familiar, Nathan purchased a daily paper and sat on one of the many sofas. Too nervous to read, he scrutinized every person who walked into the lobby. An elderly twosome stopped at the reception area and then turned in their direction. The man used a cane and was extremely pale.

"Pardon me," the man asked. "Are you Nat Edwards?"

"Why, yes, and are you Jackie Jackson?"

"Yes, I am."

After formal introductions, the two couples went into the dining room for breakfast. The women decided to get acquainted while their husbands reminisced: "Well, it seems we've changed somewhat over the years," began Jackie.

Nat answered in a laughing tone, "Only slightly!"

"What are you doing now?" Jackie inquired.

"Retired."

"Me too."

"How do you like it?" Nathan asked.

"Truthfully, it is boring."

"Yeah, I find it the same. What did you do for a living?" asked Nathan.

"Research. After high school, I went on to the state university and got a degree in biology. I joined a company called Atlas Research and worked with them until a few years ago. At that point, I was forced out," Jackie related sadly.

"Forced?"

"The company has a mandatory retirement age. After that, I tried to do some consulting work, but that quickly dwindled because of the economy. Anyway, that is where I am now. What about you?"

Nathan detailed his past and the events that had led him to his retirement. They discussed their families and the void in each of their daily lives. Meanwhile their wives conversed congenially about their children and grandchildren.

"Do you remember the day we graduated?" asked Nathan.

"Absolutely, I remember the party at Carolyn Ambrey's house and then the time we had at Fulton's Creek."

They laughed and carried on for over an hour. After breakfast, they decided to do some sightseeing together. They agreed to meet at Nathan and Marsha's car.

"Are you having fun?" asked Marsha, after she and Nathan had returned to their room.

"Absolutely! It has been a long time since I last saw Jackie and yet, it seems so recent," he pondered.

"He is certainly an interesting person and his wife is charming."

"Perhaps we can visit them sometime," suggested Nathan.

"We'll see, but let's not rush the reunion," Marsha replied.

The two men sat in the front of the vehicle while their wives shared the rear seat. "By the way, Jack, what ever happened to your brother John?"

"He died several years ago...and what about *your* sisters and brothers?"

"All dead, I am the last one left," Nathan said sadly as he started the car and exited the lot. "Where shall we go?"

"I have no idea. I have not been back since graduation. Just follow your instincts."

They turned toward town only to be amazed by the changes. The once tiny hamlet with its small locally owned shops contrasted greatly to the present bustling town. A few storefronts were familiar, but almost everything was different. Fast-food restaurants and other discount stores lined the main avenues. The corner drug store was now an oriental market and their favorite hangout had been replaced by a furniture showplace.

The car maneuvered through Katyville, as the two explorers and their wives recaptured their past. Heading up Second Avenue, a smirk crossed Jackie's face. "How about a Nizzy?"

"Perfect!" shouted Nathan.

"What on earth is a Nizzy?" asked Marsha.

"Probably the best darn chili dog in the East," replied an elated Nathan.

"We used to eat them constantly as kids," interjected Jackie.

"In fact, I've never eaten a better hot dog in the past fifty years," declared Nathan.

"You're right, none are better than Nizzy's."

After pulling into the lot, they made their way into the old building. The signs were new, but a familiar aroma filled the room. The wives found an empty booth, while the men went to order.

"Can I help you?" asked the teenager behind the counter.

"Four Nizzys, fries, and Cokes."

They waited for the uniformed adolescent to return with their order. "Ten-fifty," she said.

"Ten-fifty!" responded Nathan. "I remember the same thing costing only a few dollars."

"You're right, I recall paying a lot less for everything," agreed Jackie.

The young girl did not respond, but took their money and handed Nathan his change. They carried the food to a corner table and presented it to their wives. Jackie announced, "And now, young ladies, you are about to dine on the finest chili dog in the world."

Each ate silently and savored the legend. "Well, what do you think?" asked Jackie.

"It's very good," said Marsha reluctantly. "Excellent."

The two men were overjoyed and they reminisced further about their childhood ventures and their craving for Nizzys. As the two men returned to purchase two more, Sharon turned to Marsha. "What do you really think of Nizzys?"

"Honestly, they are nothing special. In fact, I find them quite awful."

"I agree, but I thought it was me," Sharon concurred in a whisper.

"Let's not tell the men, we wouldn't want to burst their bubbles," Marsha suggested.

After the men consumed their second Nizzys, the group strolled back to the car to continue the tour of Katyville. By mid-afternoon, they returned to their motel rooms.

Nathan went directly to the bathroom. Following several minutes of unusual quiet, Marsha knocked on the door. "Nat, are you okay?" she asked.

"I feel a little sick to my stomach. Do you have some of that medication with you?"

"I'll get it. Are you sure that is all?"

"Yes, I'm positive."

"Maybe it was the Nizzy?" Marsha ventured.

He did not respond, but took the medication from her. After swallowing the pills, he relaxed on the bed. "I don't think it was the Nizzys. Probably just the excitement; after all, I ate them for years."

She didn't answer, but watched as he slept. Picking up the phone, she called Sharon. Like Nathan, Jackie was experiencing stomach trouble. "Excitement?" Sharon scoffed. "The Nizzys are the same, but the men have changed."

T H I R T E E N

By 7 p.m. the couples met in the main lobby. Each was nicely dressed. Full of anticipation, they drove to the high school. The sound of a band vibrated as they walked to the gym entrance.

"The place certainly has changed," observed Jackie.

Nat responded, "It is a far cry from when we came here."

Small groups congregated along the path, but neither Jackie nor Nat recognized any of their former classmates. As they reached the foyer, welcoming signs were hung.

"Our year's class meets over here," said Jackie as he pointed to the far corner. They maneuvered to the reception table and found several name tags. A slender, middle-aged woman was seated behind the table. "Can I help you?" she inquired.

Nathan responded, "You must be Arlene Welson."

"Why, yes, how did you know that?"

"A lucky guess."

"And you are?"

"Nathan Edwards, and this is my wife Marsha."

"Mr. Edwards, I remember speaking to you about the reunion. I am so glad the two of you made it."

"This is Jackie and Sharon Jackson. He is a fellow classmate."

Arlene extended her hand and warmly greeted them all. "Your class is the oldest here tonight, and I am pleased several of you have made the journey. You will be seated at Table Two. A few others are inside already, so why don't you go in and get reacquainted. It is going to be a fun evening."

"Is George Baudes here yet?" asked Nathan.

"Mr. Baudes called and canceled at the last minute," replied Arlene.

"Did he give a reason?" Nathan queried.

"Something about having to care for his grandchild, but he did say he would try to reach you in the near future." Nathan was disappointed he would not be seeing his friend.

They donned their name tags and headed inside. The band was blaring as they made their way across the huge gym floor. The room was crowded as groups of former friends warmly greeted one another. To the right of the head table, Jackie noticed their table. "It looks as if someone else is there," said Marsha as they drew closer.

Another couple was already seated. "Hello, my name is John Hayes and this is my wife Janie."

Nathan introduced himself, his wife, and the Jacksons, and then asked, "I don't recall graduating with anyone named Hayes."

"That is true. It is Janie's graduating class."

"Janie, what was your maiden name?"

"Gladden."

"Gladden! Are you little Janie Gladden from Main Street."

"The one and only," she replied.

The questioning began as the three reduced their past into a few minutes. Their spouses listened and spoke among themselves. "It appears there are not too many of us still around," noted Nathan.

"Only the most stubborn and obviously the most important," quipped Jackie.

They laughed and then listened as Janie filled them in on the fates of their old friends. Death and infirmity had afflicted most not in attendance. Their discussion was broken as a tall gentleman approached the table. "May I join in the fun?"

"Certainly," said Janie.

"So this is what is left of my class?" the man asked.

"So far...but who are you, may I ask?" Nathan said.

"I'll give you a hint. I was the star quarterback on your winning football team."

"You're not Alexander Parkes?" inquired Janie, incredulous.

"Yes, I am. Here and in the flesh." He proceeded to hug each of his fellow classmates and quickly joined in the conversation. The discussion became louder and more exuberant as time passed.

"I notice there is only one more chair. Does anyone else know our missing classmate?" asked Janie.

No one had any ideas, but the dilemma was soon solved as a gray-haired woman found her way to the vacant chair. Nathan looked intently in her eyes and then smiled a knowing smile. "You are Mary Hendon. I would know you anywhere."

"That is correct. And you, of course, are Nathan Edwards," she replied.

Everyone was amazed the two readily recognized each other. Just as Marsha was about to ask, the lights dimmed and a middle-aged man strolled to center stage and introduced himself to the crowd.

"My name is Stephen Black and I am the current superintendent of schools for the district of Katyville. Let me welcome you to the reunion and I would like to introduce several others responsible for this celebration. Without them..." His speech lasted ten minutes and after the local pastor offered a brief prayer, the lights were again brightened and the gaiety continued.

The band played a mixture of songs to satisfy their many patrons. Most, however, were not even listening to the music, but rather to their newly re-found friends. Every table rekindled the past as attendees bridged their previous lives. Emotions ran from happiness and joy to extreme sadness. The older the individuals, the more somber the atmosphere.

"Tell me, Alexander, how good was your football team?" asked Marsha.

"We were excellent; both Nathan and Jackie were stars on the team. Didn't they tell you that?"

"I guess they're just modest..." she replied.

As the salad was being served, Nathan asked Marsha to dance. Holding her close, he maneuvered her around the dance floor. "Your classmates are all very nice. I am having a good time. Are you?" she asked.

"Yes, this is great."

They returned to the table and listened as Alexander continued to dominate the conversation. "After my wife died, I traveled for several years..."

"Tell me, Mary," asked Jackie. "What did you do all these years?"

"I remained in Katyville and worked as a bookkeeper until my retirement. Since I never married, my hobbies and interests filled most of my time..." Throughout the conversation she pointedly directed her conversation away from Nathan.

As soup was being served, Nathan asked Marsha, "Would you mind if I danced with Mary, for old times sake?"

"Not at all," replied Marsha.

He gently escorted his former classmate to the dance floor. He held her gingerly as they danced, "It's been a very long time, Mary, and you look as lovely as ever."

"You seem to have endured the test of time yourself," she replied.

"You never married?"

"No, I waited for the longest time, but that very special person never returned. Finally I gave up and filled my time with other interests. How is your life?"

"Quite good. I have a wonderful wife, children, and many grandchildren...I cannot get over your being here tonight."

"Why not? I did graduate you know."

"That's not what I meant. It is a very pleasant surprise," Nathan said.

"For both of us…a happy occasion." As the music ended she kissed him gently on the cheek and then followed him back to the table. They again became engulfed in the conversation. Before anyone realized it, the reunion was over. Addresses were exchanged and promises made. Each vowed to keep alive the spark that had been briefly lit. Only Alexander would be leaving the next day, so Jackie, Janie, and Nathan would still have more time to get reacquainted. Mary promised to see each of them before they left. By the time the band stopped playing, a tentative schedule was developed by the four former classmates. Each warmly said goodbye to Alexander and watched as he disappeared into the dispersing crowd. Mary was the next to go. The rest savored memories for several more minutes before returning to the motel.

Back in their room, Nathan cuddled close to his wife and kissed her tenderly on the cheek. "Thank you for coming to my reunion. I hope you were not too bored."

"Not at all, I found it fun. Sharon and I have a great deal in common and had no problem sharing experiences."

"By the way, I love you very much," whispered Nathan.

She had not heard those words in years and responded by moving closer. "I love you also."

F O U R T E E N

The ringing of the phone abruptly awoke Marsha and Nathan. An emergency had forced Janie and her husband to leave ahead of schedule. They called to say good-bye and promised to keep in touch once things had settled. After dressing, Nathan descended to the lobby and purchased the daily paper. After returning to the room, he read each page thoroughly.

"It's amazing," he said. "Prices are about the same as where we live. Except for the cost of buying a home, everything seems to be on a par."

"Why does that surprise you?" Marsha asked.

"It just does, that's all. I don't remember things being so costly here."

"Remember, that was sixty years ago."

"I guess you are correct," he admitted.

When ready, the couple walked to Room 615 and knocked.

"Come on in, the door's open," shouted Jackie from inside.

They entered and waited as Sharon finished dressing in the bathroom. After she was done, they headed downstairs for breakfast. Arlene Welson had done an admirable job handling both the reunion and organizing an optional agenda. The two couples planned on her general program.

They followed the map as it directed them through Katyville. At noon, Jackie asked "Is anyone hungry?"

"I think we could all use a lunch break," answered Marsha.

"What about a Nizzy?" inquired Jackie.

"I think we'll pass on the Nizzy," said Marsha. She turned to her husband. "My stomach is not too good today. Perhaps we can eat something bland. I hope I am not spoiling your fun…"

Knowingly, and quite appreciatively, Nathan responded, "Not at all, I vote we eat a healthy lunch." Everyone agreed and they drove to Ollie's Luncheonette. Once inside, the two men marveled at the changes. The individual booths were gone, as was the long counter. Instead, small plastic tables filled the brightly decorated area. After ordering from an ornately designed menu, Nathan and Jackie went to the men's room.

While washing, a middle-aged man entered. He looked at the two men and then began cleaning his hands. Being inquisitive, Nathan asked, "Pardon me, I wonder if I might ask you a few questions?"

"Certainly."

"When did they change Ollie's?"

"About twenty years ago. After Ollie died, his wife was forced to sell the business. Too much work for her…anyway, the Smiths from Elizabethtown bought it next. They lasted for fifteen years and then sold to the current owners. What you see was their idea. Personally, I kind of liked it the old way."

"Me too," said Nathan.

"I was just wondering. Are you two here for the reunion?" asked the man.

Jackie responded, "We are."

"I thought so. I didn't recognize either of you."

"It's been a long time for both of us. By the way, when did they change James Street?" Nathan asked.

"About ten years ago."

"Are you eating lunch here?" inquired Nathan.

"Yes, why do you ask?"

"How about joining us? We both have many questions and would appreciate a few answers," said Nathan. "By the way, what is your name?"

"Hank Silver."

"Are you related to the Silvers on Hamson Avenue?" asked Jackie.

"Relatives."

They returned to their table and introduced Hank to their wives. For the next hour, Hank detailed the past sixty years of Katyville's growth and metamorphosis. By the time he left, everyone had a comprehensive understanding of the changes.

With mixed emotions, Nathan drove the car into the Katyville High School parking lot, which was rapidly filling for the football game. Following Arlene Welson's directions, the two couples entered the main gate and received honorary passes to the game. "At least the grass is still green," remarked Jackie as they stared at the transformed field.

The Katyville band marched onto the field. After the national anthem, the Katyville High School song was played. Standing with everyone, Jackie and Nathan mouthed the words of the song.

As the exhibition game progressed, both men were amazed at the size and skill of the players. "Look at the size of that defensive line!" said Jackie.

Nathan shook his head. "Things certainly are a lot different, including the game itself. Much more complicated than when we played."

"You said a mouthful. I am glad I played when I did," commented Jackie.

By the end of the third quarter, Katyville was way ahead of its opponent; the game was a runaway. Since this was the case, the two couples left and drove back to the motel. After a quiet supper, they retired to their rooms.

FIFTEEN

With only one more day, the two couples attempted to make the best of their remaining time. They followed the suggested routes and deviated whenever the need arose. Though they did find a few more familiar sights, most of Katyville had changed. Most of their memories were relics; each segment diminished before their eyes. By 4 p.m., they realized their quest into their background was fruitless. It would and could never be the same. Silently, they returned to the motel.

Marsha decided to take a short nap and once she was asleep, Nathan went downstairs. Finding a pay phone, he quickly dialed a memorized number.

"Hello?"

"Is Mary there?"

"This is Mary. Who is this?"

"Nathan."

After a short pause, she responded, "I was hoping you would call."

"It is the first chance I've had. With all the sightseeing and all, I couldn't get to a phone."

"I understand."

"I don't know what to say. It's been such a long time," began Nathan.

"I know. It's been many years since you left Katyville and a lot of water has gone under the bridge."

"Mary, I just want to apologize..."

"Nat, there is nothing to apologize for. The past is dead and must remain that way. We both have to live for the future."

"I know, but you looked so damn beautiful the other night and it made me feel so guilty," Nathan said.

"Guilty? Over what? You made your choice and it was apparently a correct one. Your wife is lovely and seems to be a wonderful person."

"Marsha is marvelous and more than I had even expected. It's just that I feel guilty..."

"Nat, there is no reason to feel that way. Now drive carefully and if you ever return to Katyville, just promise to call."

"I promise...and I want to tell you Mary, that I still love you very much."

"I know and I love you too. Nat, do not stir up old embers, we have our memories and that must be enough. Now go to Marsha," directed Mary.

Before hanging up the receiver, he uttered once more into the phone, "I love you..." He stayed in the phone booth for several minutes to regain his composure. Nathan dried his eyes and returned to the room.

Marsha was up. "Where have you been? I was worried."

"I just went downstairs for a few minutes. I wanted to buy a magazine, but I couldn't find anything I liked." He walked to her side and pressed her slender frame to his body. She did not say a word, but offered him the comfort he desired.

SIXTEEN

Marsha started packing their clothes. "Nathan, you forgot to wear your sweater." She held it up for him.

"Well, it's too late now. Just put it in the suitcase."

"What about wearing it today?"

"I don't think so, I'll wear it at home."

She did not question his decision, and carefully placed the garment in the suitcase. Once everything was packed, they took the luggage to their car. They returned to the lobby and waited for Jackie and his wife.

Nathan purchased the daily newspaper again. He shook his head in disbelief as his previous world of memories gave way to the present. "Nothing's the same," was all he could mutter to himself.

His thoughts were interrupted by a gentle nudge. "Nathan, Jackie and Sharon are here."

He stood and smiled, "What about breakfast?"

"I am afraid Sharon and I must leave right away. It's going to be a long trip and I want to get started now."

Nathan embraced his friend. "Have a good trip and please drive carefully." They exchanged addresses and phone numbers. "Please keep in touch."

"We will and perhaps we can make arrangements to get together soon," said Jackie warmly.

"I'd like that," replied Nathan. He hugged his fellow classmate one last time, and watched as Jackie and his wife exited the lobby. Marsha took her husband's hand as he stared at the closed door.

"Come, Nathan, let's get something to eat."

As they ate, despite all of Marsha's attempts to encourage conversation, Nathan remained speechless. After paying for the meal, they walked to their room. Both inspected every nook and cranny to make sure nothing was left behind. Once the inspection was completed, they paid their bill and walked to the parking lot.

A familiar piece of paper on the ground caught Nathan's eye. He picked up the wrinkled sheet and noted that his address and phone number were written on it. "What is it?" asked Marsha.

"It is the note I gave Jackie; the one with our number and address."

"He must have dropped it."

"Probably."

"At least we have theirs," Marsha consoled. Nathan dejectedly stuffed the wrinkled note into his pocket. He steered the car out of the lot and turned into the heart of Katyville.

"Where are we going?" asked Marsha.

"I just want to see the place one last time. He drove down several streets, including the one where he had lived and played, past his former schools, and finally through the business district. "I've had enough," he said as he maneuvered the car toward the thruway.

The trip home was uneventful. They stopped several times along the way for fuel and to stretch. By midnight, they pulled into their driveway. Nathan and Marsha got out of their car and stared at the darkened exterior. "It's good to be home," said Marsha.

Nathan carried their luggage into the front hall. Looking around, he gazed at their household belongings. "You're right, it is good to be home."

SEVENTEEN

The next morning Nathan was up early. He unpacked their suitcases and started washing the dirty clothes. By the time Marsha awoke, most of the work was done. She called her children and then made breakfast. "What do you want to do today?" Marsha asked.

"I think I will take a short walk. Why do you ask? Did you have something else in mind?"

"The girls want to take me shopping, but I told them I'd let them know later."

"Go with them. I have plenty to keep me busy."

"Are you sure?"

"I'm positive. Call them right now." Sharon phoned and made preparations for the afternoon.

After she was picked up, Nathan set about working around the house. Throughout the entire day he labored as if trying to block out something. Even after Marsha's return, he worked.

The next morning he awoke very early. Gathering several items, he descended quietly to the basement. Opening the appropriate box, he neatly laid his high school sweater inside. Looking one last time at his yearbook, he lingered at Jackie Jackson's picture, and then closed the book. Sighing, he deposited the book next to his sweater and secured the box.

Returning upstairs, he turned on the television. Patiently he waited for Mr. Roye to deliver the mail. By the time Marsha entered the room, her letters were neatly piled on the dining room table.

"Nathan, do you want to go shopping with me today?"

"I don't think so; I'm kind of tired. I think I'll just sit and watch some television. By the way, could you get some snack food, there is none in the house."

Although surprised, she did not question his request; she left to buy the groceries. Nathan picked up the remote control and switched on the television. Settling back in his chair, he raised his legs on the foot stool, and began to watch his usual programs.

The Home

O N E

Repetition and routine were the only words needed to completely describe life at the nursing facility. With the exception of an occasional relative's visit, residents relied solely on one another's company for stimulation. Life passed swiftly on the structure's exterior, but inside, time was an extension of one's existence. Days were carbon copies of each other, and only hospitalization or death changed the cast of characters.

The majority of the staff were dedicated; however, as with any other employment environment, a few just put in their time and feigned relationships with the patients.

Five patients who were unimpaired congregated each day. Surrounded by desolation and gloom, they assisted one another in maintaining a semblance of sanity. Without each other, the pillars of support would have collapsed and the entire group would have faded into the general populace of desperation and disparity.

None of the five elders ever had visitors; their few distant relatives avoided the institution. Out of guilt or personal fear, the outside world circumvented the group. Each morning they would eat breakfast and then move to the large rotunda. There they waited.

Surrounded by the living dead and the continual stench of urine and feces, the tiny group hung onto their mental balance by a thread. They were, indeed, the stalwarts of their peers.

By 10 a.m., they progressed to the institution's therapy department. Though an insult to their integrity and intelligence, the five elders utilized the program to fill their time. Whether making potholders, oil paintings, or other sundry activities, each considered the actions a total waste of staffing and money.

After a couple of hours, it was back to the dining room for a typical institutional lunch. All were capable of independent function, but due to extenuating circumstances, were placed in the home. Like magnets, they clung tightly together for support.

The afternoon was spent in the rotunda once again. They read papers and books, but more importantly, they discussed current events and other pertinent and controversial subjects. An occasional visit by a church group, Girl Scout troop, or volunteers was a useful diversion to the realities of the melancholy world all experienced.

After supper, each would retire to individual rooms and by 8 p.m., all would be deeply asleep. The pattern never changed except on weekends. During that time, the therapy departments were closed and the five seniors were forced to resort to their ingenuity to cope with their environment.

Periodic disagreements occurred among them, but each fully understood their relationship, and never held any malice. For six years, the bonds solidified and only grew stronger as each member's dependency on the group intensified.

T W O

Stephen Fueller was the eldest of the group. Born ninety-four years before, he was not only remarkable for his age, but exemplified every person's dream of old age. With nearly full mental and physical capacities, he experienced no significant suggestion of pain. Though not one hundred percent, his visual and auditory acuity were more than sufficient to carry out daily functions. With no living relatives or place to go, he had been forced to reside at the nursing home.

Raised by a middle-class family, Stephen was afforded the luxury of a college education. He attended an Ivy League school and received his bachelor's degree in business administration. While working, he completed his Masters degree in finance.

He easily outlasted his four sisters and brothers. Never having married, he enjoyed a life of travel and freedom. He had visited eighty countries and was well-endowed with practical experience.

Upon retirement from a huge conglomerate as a senior vice president, he spent the remainder of his active years doing consultations and lectures. Finally he relinquished his home and admitted himself to the nursing facility. He had not expected to live as long nor did he expect to be in the physical condition his body actually enjoyed. With no one left on the outside, he was resigned to spending the remainder of his days at the institution.

The staff tended to avoid Stephen as much as possible due to his exceedingly articulate communication skills and above-average intelligence. Instead they cared for the more ill and infirmed. It was therefore easy to comprehend why Stephen was the natural spokesperson for his small group of senior citizens.

THREE

Sarah Ericmark was chronologically the next in line. At eighty-seven, she suffered only mild emphysema and asthma. Having lived with these conditions for years, she had learned to modify her life accordingly.

Born in the inner city of a large metropolis, she had become accomplished in the art of survival. Her father did his best to support their family, but a laborer's salary was far from adequate. Realizing there was only one means of escape, she married the first eligible suitor at the tender age of fifteen.

She bore three children before her husband died from a job-related injury. Forced to work, she toiled at various positions to keep her small family solvent. Her formal education terminated in fifth grade and despite her longevity, she had never learned to read or write.

One by one, her children died, finally leaving her alone. With no means of support and moderate health, she became a ward of the state and was ultimately admitted to the nursing facility for long-term care.

Sarah was attracted to Stephen and the rest of the group. Though not as naturally didactic, she contributed a great deal of common sense experience to their daily discussions.

FOUR

Inez Brown had the distinction of being the only black and sole celebrity of the group. Being raised by a famous show-business family, it was only natural that she joined their act. Working on stage was second nature and by the time she was eight, she was performing solos. She remained with her family's troupe until she met and married a fellow entertainer.

While singing in an off-Broadway production, a top director discovered her talents and signed her to star in his newest production. Instant success followed, both professionally and financially; however her relationship with her husband deteriorated. After a long and costly divorce, her first marriage was terminated.

Flamboyant living and professional achievements decorated the remainder of her active years. Four other marriages all ended painfully, and a series of countless other suitors merely satisfied her sexual desires. None lasted any length of time nor were any of substance.

She performed in various media until she reached the age of seventy-five. At that point, an extensive series of professional rejections caused her to go physically downhill. She drank heavily and started to experiment with a variety of drugs. With her money just about gone and death close at hand, her long-time family physician had her institutionalized.

Once admitted, the withdrawal process had to be accomplished; after its completion, many of her former attributes quickly returned. She joined the small group for companionship and preservation of her sanity.

F I V E

Lyndel Smythe was the only foreign-born member of the group. At eighty, he still keenly remembered many of his former escapades. An old naval wound caused him to limp badly and confined his ambulation to short distances.

After a difficult childhood and adolescence, Lyndel joined the Royal Navy until age and his ailing leg forced his retirement. During his glory years, he served aboard many a vessel and actively partook in three wars.

He loved both his liquor and his women and spent extravagantly on both during all his leaves. Even upon his retirement, he enjoyed both to the best of his ability. Never having time or the inclination to marry or seek out his remaining family, he classified himself as a loner and lived accordingly.

With no permanent roots, he traveled from place to place after leaving the military. Not an individual of high moral stature, he cared little for his female companions and only used them until he grew weary of their association. Crudeness and selfishness described his behavior.

He found himself in a state hospital after running out of both money and health. After his conditions were stabilized, he was turned over to the nursing facility. Finding no one else to speak coherently to, he joined the small group. Their initial reaction was one of rejection, but once Lyndel conformed to their unspoken conduct guidelines, he became a full-fledged member.

S I X

The final and youngest member of the group was Ann Brothers. At the age of seventy, she was a mere child compared to the other four. Her life experiences, however, were much more limited and mundane compared to the other group members.

Limited only physically by congestive heart failure, Ann was able to function independently at the facility. Her cardiac condition was successfully treated by medication, permitting her to keep up with her companions easily.

She had been born in a neighboring hospital and spent her earliest years living a few miles from the nursing home itself. Her parents raised her along with her two brothers, in a cold-water flat. She graduated from high school and went on to a nearby college. When her parents and brothers all died in a fiery disaster, she lost herself in school and then work.

Feeling endless guilt for escaping the murderous inferno, she dedicated herself to her job at the local library. There she divorced herself from life and the outside world. Vacations were never taken and holidays were usually spent alone or with a few acquaintances from her job.

When she reached the age of seventy, her entire world collapsed. A forced retirement from the library caused her immediate
mental downfall and was the spark that ignited her breakdown.
Unable to care for herself, the state had her institutionalized at the
nursing facility.

Drawn to the group for some unknown reason, she remained
subdued and passive for the longest time. As days passed, she
extended somewhat from her inner self and joined in many of their
interesting and controversial discussions.

SEVEN

A gentle snow commenced to fall as the ambulance leisurely made its way down the long driveway. Staring out the windows, the residents observed as the stretcher was lifted from the vehicle and carried into the front entrance. Those with mental capacity realized another patient was being admitted. There would be no pomp or circumstance for the newest arrival; he or she would be unceremoniously assigned a room.

It was well into the next day when the latest patient was wheeled into the rotunda. His deep brownish skin and long black hair accented his sharp facial features. With piercing eyes, he gazed at his new surroundings and evaluated his latest predicament.

Looking at the crippled and gnarled bodies before him, he was drawn to the five apparently healthy figures sitting in the rotunda. For the longest period, he simply stared at them. Finally he closed his eyes and hoped this was all a dream.

For a week the same pattern followed, though the new resident became more lethargic with each day. The nurses and other staff frequently urged him to eat. In spite of both pleas and threats, he refused to consume any more than a morsel of bread and water. He remained intrigued by the five healthy individuals and continually gazed in their direction.

Finally with every last bit of energy he could muster, he wheeled his chair to their location. As he approached, they observed his coming. He stopped within two feet of Stephen and ceased all movement. Breaking the stillness, Stephen asked, "Welcome, my friend. What is your name?" No response came from the stranger's lips. Several others of the group tried to prompt conversation, but each attempt was met with silence. Instead of pursuing the issue, and remembering Ann's first silent days in the group, they continued with their previous discussion.

Every day the intruder rolled over to the group, but never partook in any of its activities or dialogue. Accepting that the latest member to their group would not leave their presence, they wheeled him into the dining room and therapy areas with them. In both places, he sat immobile; still only a small amount of bread and water was consumed at meals.

Head nurse Henderson made her way across the dining room and stood directly before the group. Harshly addressing their newest member, she asked, "Are you eating yet?"

Noting no response forthcoming, Stephen quickly interceded. "He is doing just fine, head nurse Henderson. He eats everything on his plate and even asks for more."

"But the reports I have been receiving are..."

"They are simply not true, Missy," interjected Lyndel. "He not only eats all his food but usually takes some from all of us."

"Yes!" chimed Sarah. "We are speaking the truth."

Head nurse Henderson stared once more at the seated patient and then spoke, "I hope you are being honest with me. He is my responsibility."

"We would not make up something like this," said Inez. "The man looks better already."

"Well, we'll just have to see next week when he gets weighed." She exited the dining room.

Stephen smiled at the members of the group and then to the stranger. "Look, you must eat or you are going to get us all in a lot of trouble."

No reply. Ann picked up a spoonful of food and held it before the stranger's mouth. Looking sternly at him, she pushed the utensil to his lips. "Now eat." He returned her look then consumed the food. She fed him while the others watched. After lunch, the six seniors returned to the rotunda for the afternoon activities.

EIGHT

A slight difference in the stranger was observed by the group: Though still mute, he appeared keenly interested in their daily conversations. He never spoke, yet each member instinctively knew every word and thought was being absorbed. Ann continued to feed the newcomer and all were amazed at the voracious appetite he exhibited.

Once the weighing confirmed his progress, head nurse Henderson avoided the group entirely and showed no interest in their newest colleague. He had been generically labeled John Smith, the name learned from his hospital wristband. "John" would acknowledge the designation with an occasional nod or small sign, but an overall submissive behavior persisted.

The cohesive union among the five methodically engulfed John. He silently maneuvered himself into the tightly composed association and played a part in their daily undertakings. Ann in particular shielded him from the institution's staff and other inquisitive persons. Several government social workers visited John, with aspirations of delving into his past, but each was coldly and unresponsively greeted by John and his newfound friends. After a while, their attempted interviews ceased and the six were left alone.

NINE

Frigid winter weather forced the institution's occupants to remain inside. Once the spring and its warmer temperatures arrived, many of the patients sought the tranquility of the lawns and gardens. As in the rotunda, the six preferred to isolate themselves from the masses.

Sitting around a small pond filled with colorful koi, Stephen was leading the group in a complex dialogue over the internal mechanisms of government health practices and policies. An unfamiliar voice caused everyone to turn in the direction of John. It repeated itself, "We do not belong here!"

Every eye fell upon their formerly mute associate. Ann grasped his arm. "John!" she cried out. "You spoke!"

Peering steadily at the others, John once again spoke, "I said, we do not really belong here!"

After getting over the initial shock, Stephen asked, "John, why didn't you speak to us before?"

"Yes," inquired Inez. "After all we did for you. What is wrong with you?" John remained silent as their interrogation continued.

"Speak up! You at least owe us an explanation!" stated Ann

who probably suffered the most from this recent development.

"You made us all out as fools!" shouted Lyndel. "We were taken advantage of…that's what I think!"

Finally John spoke in his own defense, "I am sorry each of you feels the way you do; my intention was not to hurt any of you. After all, we are friends."

"But why?" asked Ann in a pleading tone.

"I will not and cannot go into the details of my life before coming here, but I will sum it up with one word: horrendous. It was beyond any description and therefore my trust in anyone was just about totally gone. It has taken me all this time to gain any confidence in our relationship and, more importantly, in myself as a worthwhile human being."

The group remained quiet as John continued, "I apologize to each of you if I have insulted or hurt you in any way, but we are each islands within ourselves. Only when we are actually ready to mix with others can it occur."

Stephen asked, "You appear to be educated. Am I correct?"

"Yes. I have studied at several universities in the past and have a post-graduate degree. That is irrelevant in my current situation. All that matters is the present and the future."

" Can you explain further?"

"As I said before, we do not belong here."

"Then where do we belong?" retorted Lyndel in an almost sarcastic tone.

"I am not sure, but we are all in fairly good physical and mental condition. If you question my hypothesis, look around at the others and you'll see what I am talking about."

"Suppose that is true," inquired Inez, "what can we do about it?"

Lyndel interjected, "This is making no sense at all. We cannot decide to leave any time we wish. There are rules!"

"Agreed!" shouted Sarah. "We must abide by the regulations."

"Let's not get too excited. John was only making a statement," said Ann.

"Besides, we are wards of the state and cannot just leave any-time we desire. Is that true, Stephen?" inquired Sarah.

"Yes, but let's all think about what has been posited here and talk about it tomorrow."

Everyone agreed to keep the meeting confidential. They also decided John should maintain his speechless charade a little longer, as they did not desire to draw any attention to themselves.

Before leaving, Ann turned to John and asked, "What is your real name?"

"Sylvester Martin Barlow."

No one questioned him any further; instead they left for the dining room.

T E N

Early the next day the six elders exited the institution and moved directly to their secluded site. Fearing reprisal from the staff, each member maintained a strict code of silence until they were out of auditory range.

As if liberated from years of anxiety and frustration, they reviewed the previous day's discussion. Sylvester remained silent throughout most of the deliberations and spoke only when directly addressed. Usually his answers were condensed and amazingly precise.

"I have given quite a lot of thought to John's, I mean Sylvester's statement and I feel it merits further consideration."

"How do we get started?" asked Sarah.

"Before we even consider a course of action, we must carefully think of every possibility and risk."

"Stephen, what will be our biggest barrier?" asked Inez.

"Probably the government and its regulations regarding geriatrics."

"What do you mean?" inquired Lyndel.

"According to the last policies I read, no elderly individual may live alone unless he or she is fully independent."

"Is that why each of us is here now?" questioned Ann.

"Exactly. Since none of us is entirely capable of functioning alone, they had no choice but to make us wards of the state and institutionalize us at this facility."

All remained quiet for a moment. Ann turned to Sylvester. "What do you think?"

"Again, I repeat, we simply do not belong here."

"That's it!" shouted Stephen. "We! That's the key."

"I do not understand," questioned Sarah.

"Let me explain." Stephen hesitated for a minute and after regaining control of his elation, he again spoke, "This must be a united effort. The word 'we' is the key to presenting our case to the administration."

"I am afraid I do not follow your thinking…" said Inez.

"It is very simple. We will ask to leave and tell them we will live together under one roof. That way, no rules will be broken and we can help one another."

"Yes!" shouted Sarah. "I can cook and Inez can—"

"Now wait just a minute. This plan will require a great deal of thought and work before we can jointly submit it to Mr. Higgens," Stephen reminded.

"I agree," said Lyndel. "After all, we all know how open-minded Mr. Higgens is."

Most smirked and waited for Stephen to continue. "Well, Sylvester, you certainly have opened a can of worms. What do you think about my proposal?"

"It seems practical and quite logical. Hopefully it will work."

They broke for lunch. A rain storm thwarted any further discussion for the remainder of the day. Instead, they played bingo and individually contemplated the proposal.

E L E V E N

During the next few weeks the group worked secretively on their strategy. Sylvester took a more assertive position and often led the discussions. Each member added to the proposal and carefully removed any flaws or rough edges from the final product. Once satisfied, they staged performances and administrative debates to prepare themselves for their confrontation with Mr. Higgens.

"Each of us appears ready. Does anyone have a question as to their task?" Stephen asked. Receiving no negative response, Stephen sent word through the staff that a meeting with Mr. Higgens was requested.

Several days later, head nurse Henderson approached the group in the rotunda. Without hesitation she attacked. "What is this all about?"

"What are you talking about?" asked Stephen in a calm and composed tone.

"Don't give me that crap! You know damn well! What is this meeting with Higgens all about?"

"Oh, that meeting. We have several things to discuss with him, that's all."

"Then you should have spoken to me first. You should know by now a protocol must be followed. How do you think this incident makes me look in the eyes of the administration?"

Remaining the diplomat he was, Stephen replied, "The meeting has nothing to do with you or the home itself. It is a personal matter that must be answered by an administrative head. We realize you are exceedingly interested in our overall well-being, but the subject does not fall within your scope of expertise. Should it have, then we would have come directly to you and would not have bothered Mr. Higgens at all. We all certainly realize how busy he must be and unless we felt this meeting was not vital to our interest, we surely would not have asked him to see us."

Noting a flicker of weakness, the senior citizen pursued his convincing justification. "We never intended to blemish your credibility by our apparent lack of protocol; however, you must realize we have been institutionalized for quite some time and perhaps are not totally aware of the proper channels that should have been followed. Please accept our deepest apologies."

The nurse stammered for a few moments and then spoke, "I guess I misunderstood your intentions…but just remember to let me know the next time you decide to do anything like this."

"Absolutely," replied Stephen. "Please forgive us for the trouble we have caused you."

She started to walk away, but stopped. "By the way, Mr. Higgens will see you tomorrow at 1 p.m. I will take you down to his office personally." No one replied.

When she had left, Stephen asked, "It appears we will get our chance. Is everyone sure they know their parts?" All nodded in response. "Then may I suggest we enjoy the day, for tomorrow our very futures are on the line."

T W E L V E

The trip to Mr. Higgens' office seemed to take forever. Head nurse Henderson pushed Sylvester's wheelchair as she led the group through the facility's passageways. Reaching the elevator, they descended to the first floor. Here, along with the rest of the administrative offices, was the one that belonged to Mr. Higgens. It was as if they had arrived in a different world; the aroma of death and despair was not discernible. Everywhere youth and life blossomed.

Making their way along the lengthy, brightly colored corridor, the seniors were awestruck by the cheerful atmosphere. Staff members stared as the small group of elders maneuvered their way through the labyrinth of rooms and cubicles. No one spoke as they forged ahead.

Finally reaching the main lobby, head nurse Henderson said, "Sit here until I return." Without replying, all sat on the plastic-covered chairs and waited. The chief of internal security watched the six seniors from his central office. Surmising that none had any intention of escaping, he returned to his work.

Minutes later, head nurse Henderson returned. "Mr. Higgens is ready. Follow me." Without questioning, they followed her to the administrator's office. The facility's executive sat behind his huge mahogany desk.

"Please make yourselves comfortable. I just want to acquaint myself with a few small things." He examined the patient charts on his desk and then said, "My name is Harold Higgens and, as you already know, I am the executive administrator of this facility. I apologize that I do not know each of you by name, but time does not permit me the luxury of meeting and knowing every resident in our facility."

They listened politely as Higgens continued, "Head nurse Henderson?"

"Yes, Mr. Higgens."

"Why don't you return to your floor and I will call you when we are finished. I do not think you will be needed for this meeting."

"As you wish, Mr. Higgens." She walked out the door. She had hoped to remain and see what all the secrecy was about, but she was confident she would find out in due time.

Glancing at his clock, Higgens asked, "Now, please tell me what this is all about. I must get to another meeting within the hour."

All eyes turned to Stephen, their delegated spokesperson. Mustering all his communicative experience and skills, he painstakingly selected each word. "Mr. Higgens, first we would like to thank you for listening to us. All of us are aware of the tremendous time restrictions you have and are deeply honored you decided to hear our predicament."

The executive looked impatiently at the wall clock and then to his desk. Sensing the campaign was in jeopardy before it had even begun, Stephen took the offensive. "We are here to request permission to leave this facility and live independently."

Startled, Higgens remained silent as the senior citizen launched his assault. "We have conducted a careful analysis of our personal and joint financial income and assets, and are certain we would have little difficulty sustaining our lives and monetary obligations. We have brought a copy of that analysis for your inspection." He placed several pieces of paper on the administrator's desk. The group watched as Higgens picked up the information and thoroughly inspected the contents.

Placing them back on his desk, Higgens stated, "I am very impressed with your undertaking and everything appears to be exactly as you have described; however you must realize my responsibilities to this facility and to every one of its residents."

"Mr. Higgens," interjected Sarah. "We are human beings just like you—not just old relics. While we continue to exist, all of us must have a reason to live. Shutting us up in an institution does not solve our problems, it only pushes them aside."

"Yes," said Inez. "We have certain needs and requirements that must be fulfilled. We should not be treated as caged animals."

"But you are provided with food, shelter, and medical needs. All of you are given complete care by the government. It is your right as a senior citizen—and our responsibility to provide it."

"That is wonderfully spoken; however when was the last time you went upstairs and observed the empty shells of life that exist within these walls?" asked Inez.

"Well…." Higgens muttered defensively.

"Well, nothing," interrupted Lyndel. "It is the most gruesome and depressing place. We smell death daily and are wasting what valuable time we have left by remaining."

"All of us are physically and mentally capable. We are prepared to help one another," stated Sarah.

Stephen then spoke, "Mr. Higgens?"

"Yes."

"May I ask you a personal question?"

"It all depends on the content."

"How old are you?"

"I am fifty-eight. Why do you want to know?"

"Do you realize that under the law, in twelve years, you could be sitting on this side of the desk?" Higgens slumped backward in his chair. Stephen jumped ahead. "Yes, Mr. Higgens, it is a shock, isn't it? Years ago, every one of us thought life would last forever and that our day would never come, but it does and you are no different. All we are asking for is the sacred right to live independently."

The administrator eased forward in his chair and stared at his hands. "I see your viewpoint and sympathize with your cause; however you must realize my hands are tied. The current rules clearly state no choice; everyone over the age of seventy must be institutionalized if he or she is not fully capable of functioning independently."

"That is not totally true!" interrupted an authoritative voice. Every eye turned to Sylvester as he continued to speak, "According to the Federal Statutes, there exists an exception to the rule. If you will look in the Federal Policies Concerning Geriatric Care, Volume 12, Section 55, under the current regulations, a geriatric patient has the right of appeal. Besides, the laws concern solely individuals, not groups. Gold versus the Federal Government awarded a similar case in favor of the plaintiff."

Higgens looked at the others and then to Sylvester. "You are Mr. Smith?"

"I was admitted under that name."

"Is that your real name?"

"No, my given name is Sylvester Martin Barlow."

"Sylvester Martin Barlow! Are you the Barlow who developed the current government regulations on geriatric care and has worked on the President's Advisory Board on Aging?"

"I have been active in the past on several of those endeavors," admitted Sylvester.

Everyone gasped at the revelation; Sylvester humbly assumed control of the meeting. "The right of appeal does exist and can be exercised by this group as the mechanism for our release. To activate the process, formal application must be filed to the local board as soon as possible. They, upon receipt of the papers, have only fifteen days in which to act. Under the current law, they must hold a formal hearing to discuss the matter."

"Suppose they do not act within the fifteen-day period?"

inquired Higgens.

"Then, according to the case I have previously cited, the government loses automatically."

"So there is actually a way," declared Ann.

"Yes, but we must operate within the current guidelines of the law," Sylvester reminded everyone. Looking directly at Higgens, the senior citizen continued, "We will require certain privileges and rights if this request is to be met successfully. I will require the use of your reference library and any up-to-date government literature."

"Certainly, Mr. Barlow."

"Can I count on some secretarial assistance if needed?"

"I will assign a full-time office worker to you, and furthermore you can use any other staff member whenever needed."

Stephen interrupted the negotiations, "Mr. Higgens, why did you change your mind and decide to help us?"

"For two reasons: First, I was and still am, a great admirer of Mr. Barlow. And secondly, twelve years is a very short time!"

They conversed a while longer. Higgens then phoned their floor and requested that head nurse Henderson return to his office. Upon her arrival, the charge nurse was astounded to find the entire group joking and chatting.

"Head nurse Henderson!" Higgens called out excitedly as she entered the room.

"Yes, Mr. Higgens."

"I would like to institute the following orders as quickly as possible. Please change all of Mr. Smith's records to the name Mr. Sylvester Martin Barlow. Every member of this group is to have total access to the entire facility at all times. This includes the offices on this floor when requested." Turning to Barlow, Higgens added, "It would indeed be my privilege to assist you in preparation of your case. If you would have me?"

"Certainly," Barlow responded.

Head nurse Henderson was at a loss for words. She dutifully led the assemblage back to their floor. Each elder retired to their room and contemplated the day's events, and what was about to unfold. Everyone realized more than their own futures were at stake: They had opened Pandora's box.

THIRTEEN

The following morning, when the group found their way to the rotunda, Sylvester was already there preparing the day's agenda. All were astonished by the metamorphosis: His wheelchair gone, Sylvester stood tall and stately amidst his colleagues. He was clean-shaven, well groomed, and neatly dressed, even in his institutional attire.

As each person arrived, he delegated a vital assignment. There was no animosity or resentment as Sylvester outlined their antici-pated course of action. Stephen accepted his more passive role and recognized his limitations compared to his more experienced and gifted colleague.

By mid-morning, books were littered atop several neighboring tables. The six elders busily collected the documentation to com-plete the formal appeal application. Head nurse Henderson and several other staff members watched in astonishment as the group labored in perfect harmony. The staff watched as Sylvester skillful-ly maneuvered through the matrix of documents, dissecting abstracts. They all did their share to the best of their abilities and with tremendous enthusiasm. Sarah's inability to read or write did not limit her capacity to assist the group, as her assignments capitalized on her strengths and not her weaknesses.

At the appointed hour, head nurse Henderson came to the table. "Are all of you ready?"

"Yes," said Stephen. "I believe we are prepared to go." He looked at Sylvester, who nodded confidently. They followed her along the hallways until they reached Mr. Higgens' office.

Once inside, they were greeted warmed by the administrator and another person. As head nurse Henderson was about to depart, Sylvester spoke, "I would appreciate it if Ms. Henderson was present at our meetings." He did not go into any explanations or reasoning for his request. She positioned herself between Inez and Lyndel.

"I would like to introduce our facility's primary attorney and legal counselor, Mr. Edward Bailey."

The stoic lawyer nodded to each member as they were introduced until it was Sylvester's turn. At that point, he smiled broadly. "It is, indeed, my pleasure and privilege to make your acquaintance. Your texts have been established standards for years and your briefs are still used by the highest of courts."

"I thank you for the compliments and for your assistance," replied Sylvester.

"I only hope I can aid you in some small way. After all, you are the world's expert in geriatric policies."

Handing Higgens several pieces of paper, Barlow spoke, "I would appreciate if both of you would review our work and let me know what you think of it."

The two men sat next to one another and examined the document. After a few minutes, Edward Bailey shook his head. "It is by far the best piece of writing I have seen in my twenty-two years of practicing law. Exceptionally done! There is nothing I can either add or subtract that would enhance its quality. I think it is perfect as is."

All in attendance grinned at Sylvester. Even head nurse Henderson saw him differently: Instead of an elderly, feeble shell, she observed a vibrant, intellectual being.

"I will have my secretary type it up immediately and send it off tomorrow morning," Higgens offered.

"I'd like to review the finished work before mailing it to the government," said Barlow.

"Certainly. I will bring it upstairs personally by midday."

Directing his question to Mr. Bailey, Sylvester asked, "Could you arrange to have copies of the latest geriatric court decisions brought to me as soon as possible?"

"Consider it done, you will have them by tomorrow."

"Thank you."

Bailey continued, "And by the way, I will volunteer both myself and the full services of my offices and associates to assist you in this appeal."

"Thank you, we are grateful. I will call upon you if necessary."

They stood and shook hands. Head nurse Henderson led them through the now-familiar hallways of the first floor. Staff members waved as the contingency walked by, for word had spread of their endeavor. Periodically one would stop and speak to them, but nurse Henderson maintained decorum and ushered them along.

F O U R T E E N

Trying to sequester themselves from the perils that lay ahead, after lunch the group went outside to relax in the warm sun. Inwardly, each was escaping the despondency of the institution. Sitting by the small pond, they watched as small, brilliant fish darted along the water's surface.

No one spoke of the day's happenings, nor did anyone quiz Sylvester about his mysterious past. Instead conversation was directed toward inconsequential subjects.

Several hours later, head nurse Henderson walked hesitantly toward them. "I have been looking for all of you for quite some time."

Stephen quickly replied, "This is our usual spot during the warm weather."

"It is quite delightful here...do you mind if I join you for a few minutes?"

"It would be our pleasure," said Inez. "Isn't the pond relaxing?"

Sitting next to Sylvester, nurse Henderson answered, "Yes, I always have had an attraction toward water and aquatic life."

The group remained unsure of the head nurse's intentions. Slowly, each member resumed their previous conversation, with head nurse Henderson adding sporadically to the subjects. When she was ready to leave, she turned to Sylvester and asked, "Why did you request that I remain at today's meeting?"

"I admire your professionalism and felt you could be of assistance to our cause," he replied.

"Thank you," she said softly. "Thank you very much for your trust and confidence." With that, she returned to the building.

F I F T E E N

Higgens decided all further preparations be performed on the facility's first floor. He felt confidentiality could be better controlled and the group would have better access to reference materials and personnel. To ensure these objectives, he assigned two large suites exclusively for these purposes. These areas were classified as restricted.

The executive solicited head nurse Henderson to temporarily abdicate her supervisory position and dedicate her working hours to assist the group. There was no deliberation; she accepted the post instantly.

Higgens himself delegated his daily duties and responsibilities to his many subordinates, so his time could be better spent helping the group. Innately he felt it was not their fight alone, but his as well. Besides the fact he could be in their place in twelve years, he saw the opportunity to make a name for himself.

After the appeal was typed, it was submitted to the entire group for final approval. Though the ultimate approval would have to come from Sylvester, he insisted everyone read the document and suggest modifications. It took hours for the process to be concluded, but after it was done, all had agreed on the end product.

Once signed by every member, Higgens personally delivered the papers to the appropriate authorities. By Sylvester's insistence he demanded a signed delivery statement, and placed this voucher within the institution's vault for safekeeping. Satisfied that their initial offensive had been accomplished, they relaxed over supper and readied themselves for the next step.

"What was their reaction when they received the papers?" asked Stephen.

"Very calm and, in fact, exceedingly businesslike. No one present appeared even surprised by the appeal," reported Sylvester.

"Did they give you any indication as to their plans?" inquired Ann.

"None whatsoever. They simply signed the receipt, read the documents, and literally closed the door in Higgens' face."

"Sylvester," asked head nurse Henderson. "What do you think of their response?"

"Typical, almost exactly what I expected."

"What do you mean?" asked Sarah.

"The papers were accepted by the lower echelon of government workers; it will take some time for the documents to travel through the red tape. Once they reach the proper authorities, then I expect a response."

"How long will that take?" questioned Inez.

"Probably a few days. Remember, you should never underestimate your opponent, especially in this case. After all, they are holding all the trump cards, but I can assure you the answer will come within the fifteen-day deadline!"

"What if they miss the deadline?" quizzed Lyndel.

"It will not occur; they are too smart to allow it."

"What shall we do next?" asked Higgens.

"Start our defense."

"Shall I call Ed Bailey?" Higgens offered.

"Not yet. There is still a great deal of work to do before his skills are needed. Just ask him to send all the available literature he has on the Farina v. Health Systems case."

"Is it important to our cause?" asked Stephen.

"I am not sure, but I recall it may offer some support on our behalf."

They conversed for hours before leaving the conference room. Prior to departing, head nurse Henderson insisted on being called by her first name, Rose. Everyone agreed and made arrangements to convene earlier than normal the next morning. The defense had to be readied and honed, for time was short and there was still a great deal to do.

SIXTEEN

The government's response was more expeditious than even Sylvester had expected. Within three days, a federal courier hand-delivered the reply to Higgens. He carried it inside and placed it on the large table. Everyone stared at the large, greenish envelope. Finally Sylvester picked it up and gave it to Stephen.

"Please read it to the group," he requested.

After carefully opening the envelope, he adjusted his glasses and read loudly so everyone in the room could easily hear every word.

"The Right of Appeal has been formally approved by the Fifth District Health Commissioner and the Department of Geriatric Policies. The hearing will be held at the Fifth District Courthouse at 10:30 a.m., eight days after receipt of this memorandum. Judge Malcolm Withers will reside at the bench and Robin B. Bradford will represent the government. The defendants may select any legal defender of their choice. The following defendants are to be present at that time: Stephen Fueller, Sarah Ericmark, Inez Brown, Lyndel Smythe , Ann Brothers, and Sylvester Barlow. Failure to appear by either side will constitute forfeiture of the case."

No one spoke as everyone absorbed the contents of the letter.

Sylvester took the paper from Stephen and silently reread the document.

"What do you think?" asked Stephen.

"It is exactly how it should have been handled by their side."

"But they gave us only eight days to prepare."

"I expected less."

"What shall we do?"

"The best we can."

Higgens then questioned Sylvester, "Have you ever heard of their attorney?"

"Yes. Robin Bradford is probably the finest government attorney concerning geriatric policies and laws. He sat on the President's Council on Aging and has served as an advisor to several of the country's finest and most prestigious law schools."

"Why him?"

"The government probably does not wish to lose this decision and will use it as an example for others who try this method of appeal."

Inez nervously asked, "What about the judge? Will he be fair?"

"Just remember he is a federal judge who has nothing to win or lose from this case. It is usually expected that this type of magistrate will automatically side with the government's position."

"What are we to do?" cried Ann. "It seems so hopeless."

"We have eight days to adequately prepare our strategy. That is all we can do. The rest is out of our hands." Sylvester thought for a brief moment and then spoke to Higgens, "Please ask Ed if he can stop by tomorrow. There are several things I would like to discuss with him concerning the Farina case."

Higgens nodded and immediately called Bailey. The rest of the group, including Rose, started their designated tasks. For the remainder of the day, they toiled.

SEVENTEEN

Ed Bailey arrived early the next day and sat between Sylvester and Higgens. Several of the senior partners of Bailey, Bailey, and Watzer volunteered to assist the group, and the room filled quickly. To expedite the process, individual task forces were established. Each was delegated specific responsibilities. The overall direction was designated by Ed Bailey or Sylvester. Every few hours, each division would report its status to the group at large. Any strategic modifications would be formulated and necessary reassignment of tasks emanated from these discussions.

The only non-lawyer within the primary team was Rose Henderson. She sat quietly at Sylvester's side and listened intently to the legal terminology bantered about among the participants. The biggest surprise was the ease with which Sylvester assumed control and effortlessly handled even the most difficult of chores. Every partner heeded the senior member's interpretations and little disagreement ensued.

By the end of the day, every group had accomplished a tremendous amount. Before breaking, the alliance relaxed and spoke freely among themselves. Age posed no barrier as individuals shared their thoughts. Finally Sylvester got the entire group's attention. "Ed, on behalf of myself and my other associates, I would like to thank you and your partners for today's assistance. Without you, we certainly could not have come this far. It has been my personal pleasure to review the various briefs and to learn from your experience and expertise."

Ed responded for his firm and those attorneys present: "I thank you, but perhaps you did not comprehend our intent: We plan to be here the rest of the week and will also attend the appeal if necessary."

"But what about your practice?" queried Barlow.

"Junior partners can successfully handle the workload. It is not every day any of us gets an opportunity to work with an attorney of your status. Therefore it is all of us who should be thanking you for the privilege."

Sylvester was visibly honored and looked to Stephen for help. To relieve his friend, the elderly gentleman said, " I am very tired, as I am sure each of you must be. I suggest we resume early tomorrow morning."

E I G H T E E N

The days passed too swiftly, and despite all their preparation there appeared to be insufficient time. Extensive research was performed and defensive arguments were formulated. At 3 p.m. on the final day, Harold Higgens asked for everyone's attention. He gestured to Rose who exited the room. Minutes later, she and several aides returned, each one carrying several brightly colored, wrapped packages. Smiling, the administrator watched as each defendant was given at least two boxes.

"On behalf of the employees of our facility and those of Bailey, Bailey, and Watzer, I would like to present each of the plaintiffs with a small gift. It is our way of wishing you well, and perhaps assisting a cause that will ultimately affect all of our lives." Grinning, he added, "Please open your gifts."

Broad smiles creased the faces of each senior citizen as the presents were exposed. Every box contained new clothing. The men received new suits, shoes, ties, socks, and shirts while the women's boxes revealed a stylish dress, stockings, shoes, and matching bag. Every piece was beautifully coordinated. The entire staff beamed as the elderly residents stared in disbelief at their new-fashioned attire.

"No one can say we will lose this case on our looks," quipped Ed Bailey.

"With such an impressive group, there is no way we can be defeated!" added Rose.

Harold Higgens said, "I have arranged for the facility's barber and hairdresser to be here within a few minutes. Each of you is to have your hair styled and groomed."

"But there is much more to do," objected Stephen mildly.

"Just relax. After all, each of you must present yourselves in near-perfect condition. Do you agree, Sylvester?"

"I believe you have a valid point, Harold. We will all be judged by our appearance as well as our case. If we are not ready now, then we never will be," he conceded.

The group exited while Higgens and Bailey's staff finalized the plans for the next day.

N I N E T E E N

A long line of limousines waited by the nursing home's entrance. Rose Henderson led the group through the main doorway and accompanied them to their designated vehicles. For Stephen and the others, this was the first time in years they had left the facility's grounds. In culture shock, they stared at the scenery as the cars made their way out of the driveway and into the main stream of traffic.

Sylvester never raised his head, but concentrated steadily on his documents. Bailey and Higgens sat in respectful silence as the older attorney mentally prepared himself for the upcoming event.

The trip terminated in front of a gigantic marble courthouse. The structure peered downward as the stately contingency made their way up a long flight of wide stairs and into the main foyer.

They were stopped by a security guard. "May I help you?"

Bailey took control of the situation: "Yes, could you please tell me in which courtroom the Government v. Geriatrics is being held."

Glancing at his clipboard, the guard replied, "Room Three on the first floor. Go down the hallway and take a sharp left at the end. The courtroom will be on your right."

Following the guard's instructions, the now substantial crowd walked until they stood before a colossal pair of wooden doors. "Is everyone ready?" asked Bailey. All but Sylvester nodded affirmatively. Opening the doors, they walked inside. "Please take these seats here until we see what is about to occur," instructed Bailey. He took Sylvester aside. "Are you nervous?" he asked.

"Not really, but it has been a very long time since I have been in a courtroom."

"What do you want me to do once we start?"

"I am not sure, let's just see what transpires," the seasoned lawyer responded.

Minutes later, the government's attorneys arrived and seated themselves on the other side of the room. Noticing Bailey, the chief prosecutor walked in his direction. "Mr. Bailey, my name is Robin Bradford. I will be representing the federal government in this matter. It is a pleasure to meet you, but I do look forward to a quick session..." He stopped speaking as he became aware of the elderly man to Bailey's left. He studied the individual for a second and then spoke, "Sylvester, is that you?"

Unflinching, Barlow replied, "Yes, Robin, it is I."

"My God!" the government's chief attorney said. "Where have you been and what are you doing here?"

"Where I have been is a very long story, but it appears I will be your opposing attorney."

"What!" shouted Robin as he turned toward Bailey for confirmation.

"I am afraid he is telling the truth. I am only acting as his assistant," verified Bailey.

"But this can't be! Sylvester, tell me this is some sort of joke..."

"I wish I could, but those are the facts."

Robin did not respond, but appeared shaken up. He excused himself and hurriedly joined his colleagues in conference on the other side of the chamber.

Bailey asked, "How you do know him?"

"It is a long story and now is not the time to go into the details. Certainly more pressing issues are at stake."

Before either could say another word, the judge entered and

called the hearing to order. He signaled for Bailey and Sylvester as well as Bradford and his assistant to approach the bench.

"Are we ready to begin?"

"Judge Withers?"

"Yes, Mr. Bradford, what is it?"

"I am deeply concerned about my objectivity in dealing with this case."

"I'm afraid I do not understand. Why are you making this statement now. Don't you think you should have thought about it before. What is your problem, Mr. Bradford?"

Looking at Sylvester for a moment, he then spoke, "Well, it's just that I have personally known the opposing attorney in the past and this might represent a conflict of interest."

"How?"

"Well, Mr. Barlow and I have served together on several government committees and he, in fact, was one of my instructors in law school."

"Is this true?"

Sylvester responded, "Yes, your Honor."

"I see. Mr. Barlow, what is your full name?"

"Sylvester Martin Barlow."

The judge leaned back. "Are you *the* Sylvester Martin Barlow?"

"I believe I am the one you may have heard of with regard to the field of geriatrics and the law."

"Are you the primary defense attorney for this case?"

"Judge Withers, I am donning two hats during this trial. I will be the primary attorney, as well as one of the plaintiffs."

"It seems, Mr. Bradford, you have two choices at this point, since I will not permit a delay for this particular case. You can try the case with total honesty and objectivity, or the government can forfeit the decision."

Understanding the full repercussions of Wither's statement, Bradford realized he had only one choice: "Let the case begin." He glanced at Sylvester and then returned to his table to begin the trial.

TWENTY

Bradford's introductory offensive was an attempt to discredit the credibility of the plaintiffs. Stephen, Lyndel, and Inez were interrogated during the first session. One by one, Bradford questioned, probed, and attacked their testimonies. Each defendant handled the situation easily and answered every question accurately and with great detail. Barlow surmised that the government's lawyers had done quite a bit of research; the lines of inquiry were precise and extremely factual. He and Bailey said little.

A few objections were raised, but most were quickly rejected by Withers. Since the hearing did not necessitate a jury, great care had to be taken in handling the lone decision-maker.

By midday, Withers called for an hour break. After he and the government's attorneys had left the room, Barlow spoke to his fellow plaintiffs, "The three of you did a superb job on the stand."

"Are you sure?" asked Inez. "I was afraid I would say the wrong thing." Reassuring her, Bailey added, "Your testimony was great. We couldn't have asked for more."

"Why don't all of you go downstairs and have some lunch. Ed and I will join you in a few minutes. There are a few things we must discuss." Sylvester suggested.

After they left, Bailey, his partners, and Sylvester conversed freely. "What did you really think?" questioned Ed.

"Bradford is a great attorney and he is using his God-given skills to the fullest. I also feel Withers will be of no help to us at all. Has anyone ever faced him before?" asked Sylvester.

One of Ed's partners answered affirmatively. "I lost a small case years ago in one of his courts. At that time, he was a lower court judge and his decisions always favored the government. He was certainly not the ideal selection from our point of view...."

"Well, there is little we can do now under the circumstances. We'll just have to do the best we can." They adjourned and ate lunch with the others. Bailey excused himself and left the building.

As Judge Withers called the afternoon session to order, a new dimension engulfed the courtroom: Dozens of reporters overflowed the gallery. Noticing the change, Withers instilled control. "This is my courtroom and I expect no commotion from any of the spectators. This is not a sideshow and I will not tolerate anything that disrupts these proceedings. Does everyone fully understand?"

Turning to Bradford, he then said, "The government can now resume where it left off during our last session."

The lawyer called Sarah to the stand and started his fact-filled attack on her background and credibility. She held up nicely for quite some time but started to buckle toward the end. Once again, the two attorneys watched as Bradford worked. Ann was next. After being sworn in, another attack ensued. Unlike Sarah, she remained under strict control and answered every question with dazzling aplomb. At 4 p.m., Withers stopped the hearing and ordered a resumption at 10:00 a.m. the next morning.

While in the car, Sylvester turned to Ed, "Did you have anything to do with getting the reporters here?"

Bailey smiled broadly and looked out the window. "Sylvester," he said, "Let's just say I am cashing in a few previously owed favors. I think their attendance may affect how Withers handles the situation."

"A brilliant move," replied Sylvester. "Excellent."

Bailey watched intently as the nursing home drew nearer.

TWENTY-ONE

Sylvester called his first witness. Head nurse Henderson nervously approached the bench and after being sworn in, sat on the hard
wooden chair that occupied the witness box.

"Tell us, Ms. Henderson, if you would, your occupation and
present place of employment."

"I am a charge nurse at the government's local nursing facility."

"Could you please tell the court exactly what your responsibilities are."

"I am fully accountable to the administrator for the health and
well-being of the patients that reside on my particular floor."

"Therefore, is it safe to say you are aware of each patient's condition?"

"Absolutely; they are all under my constant care."

"Do you know the plaintiffs in this case, including me?"

"Yes."

"How long have you known them?"

"Different lengths of time."

"Would you say each is fully capable of caring for himself or
herself in an independent situation?"

Bradford shouted, "Your Honor, I object! The counselor is expecting this nurse to provide the court with objective material she is not trained to give. She is neither a physician nor a board-certified social worker. Her degree is in nursing."

"Is Mr. Bradford alluding that Ms. Henderson is not capable of providing the members of this court her professional opinion?" Barlow inserted quickly.

Withers slammed his tiny hammer downward and asked them to approach the bench. "I told both of you I expect no showy displays. This is a federal hearing and not a public shouting match." He hesitated only momentarily, "I agree with Mr. Bradford. Though the witness is a professional nurse, she is not trained in evaluating the independence capabilities of the patients under her charge."

Barlow redirected his question, "Ms. Henderson, do you feel the six plaintiffs are capable of living jointly outside the facility?"

"Yes."

"Thank you, Ms. Henderson, for your time and assistance." The charge nurse stepped down and smiled meekly at Sylvester. "I would like to call as my next witness, Mr. Harold Higgens."

After Higgens was seated, Barlow exposed the administrator's educational background and expertise. "Mr. Higgens, as the executive of your facility, I am sure time does not permit you to adequately evaluate every patient."

"That is true."

"Then how do you obtain this information?"

"From my charge nurses."

"You mean from professionals like Ms. Henderson?"

"Absolutely. Without their assistance, it would be impossible to know details about any of the residents."

"So in your professional opinion, Ms. Henderson is fully capable of evaluating a patient's mental and physical status?"

"Yes."

"Thank you, Mr. Higgens. Oh, I'm sorry; I forgot one last question. Have you come into personal contact with the six plaintiffs at your facility?"

"Many times."

"In your professional judgment, do you feel they could jointly live in an independent structure away from the nursing institution with relative safety and few problems?"

"Absolutely."

"Thank you once again. I turn my witness over to Mr. Bradford for cross-examination."

"I have no questions, your Honor." With that, Higgens watched as the trial proceeded. Shortly after, Withers called a recess for lunch.

During the break, Bailey met with the reporters. He answered many of their questions about the plaintiffs, but refused to discuss any topic pertinent to the outcome of their case. Sylvester abstained from the interviews, and instead sat with his friends while they ate.

Judge Withers called the session to order and asked both sides to conclude their presentations. Barlow rose from his chair. "I would like to call Robin Bradford to the stand." Aghast at the request, Withers questioned his reasoning.

"To establish an explicit case for myself and my fellow plaintiffs, it is imperative that Mr. Bradford testify. After all, he co-authored many of the laws the government is still utilizing today."

Noting that Barlow's request was appropriate, the judge unhappily relented. As soon as the attorney sat in the witness stand, the elderly counselor began his questioning.

"Mr. Bradford, could you please tell the court a little about your background in the field of geriatrics."

"I have studied the subject quite extensively and have been instrumental in writing much of our current legislation."

"What does your formal education consist of?"

"My undergraduate degree is in political science and I obtained my law degree from Harvard University."

"Could you please tell the court of my relationship with you during that time?"

"You were my professor and mentor."

"How did you come to specialize in geriatric laws?"

Hesitating, Robin responded, "From a series of law school programs available to forthcoming graduates."

"Could you tell me who taught the courses?"

"You did."

"And how did you obtain your first job in geriatric law?"

"From you."

"Would you say I have an understanding of today's geriatric law and fully comprehend its impact upon society?"

"You are probably still the greatest living authority on the subject and yes, I feel you have a complete understanding of the topic."

"If I told you some of the current laws were inappropriate, what would be your response?"

Withers interrupted and disallowed the question. Barlow then asked another question. "Mr. Bradford, do I really belong in a nursing facility?"

"Not from what I see here."

"But the current law states every person over seventy must be institutionalized if he or she is not fully capable of functioning independently. Is that not true?"

"Yes."

"Therefore, if I do not belong in an institution because of my existing mental and physical condition, then there must be a flaw in the current law. Is that not true?"

Withers tapped his hammer on the tabletop and reprimanded Sylvester for this form of questioning. "Mr. Bradford, is there any law on the books that prevents several senior citizens from residing together and caring for themselves?"

"The present regulations pertain only to individuals and not groups of citizens. No law prevents them from doing so unless they are physically or mentally unfit."

"Who would determine their fitness?"

"Various professionals are available for such an assessment."

214

"Professionals like head nurse Henderson and Harold Higgens, the facility's chief executive?"

Realizing he had been trapped, he submissively responded, "Yes, I suppose both would qualify."

"Mr. Bradford, how old are you?"

"I am sixty-three years old."

"Sixty-three," said Sylvester. "That gives you only seven more years…. Thank you Mr. Bradford, I have no further comments at this point."

Robin looked admirably at his former teacher and friend. Sylvester had beautifully orchestrated his position and that of the other plaintiffs and yet, the senior attorney had not blemished the government's lawyers.

"Tomorrow will be our last day. Mr. Bradford, will you be able to finish on time?"

"Yes, your Honor, my closing statement is quite concise."

T W E N T Y - T W O

As the final day's session started, Bradford approached the bench. "Judge Withers, may I speak freely?"

"Certainly."

"It is the contention of myself and the other federal attorneys that this case be awarded in favor of the plaintiffs. In all clear conscience, we feel the law is inappropriate and more importantly, seriously flawed."

Glancing at the plaintiffs occupying the chamber, the judge spoke, "It seems both sides are finished presenting their material; I will return within the hour and render my final verdict."

He exited the room. Bradford gazed with great admiration at Sylvester and smiled. In his heart, he knew Barlow was correct.

TWENTY-THREE

There was little interaction among the participants as they nervously awaited the outcome. Barlow wished this procedure had called for a jury trial, but he could not argue the point because he had co-authored the entire protocol. He even found some humor in being a victim of his own doing. After the supreme effort of the week before, now all anyone could do was wait.

Bailey pulled the reporters aside and was providing them with specific details of the regulations governing geriatrics. Many were appalled as the rules were described. For each member of the press, the lawyer distributed copies that itemized the materials Sylvester had exposed.

The door to the rear of the chamber opened and every eye followed as Judge Withers returned to his seat. He cleared his throat before speaking.

"I have given much thought to what has transpired over the past few days. This appeal's hearing is unique in that it encompasses the originators of an existing regulation with one on either side of the case."

"There are actually two factors that must be considered: One is the law itself and the other is the actual appeal by the plaintiffs. As far as the law is concerned, it is not my place to judge if it is accurately written or fair. Checks and balances within our federal government achieve that purpose. I can only apply what is actually written and make my decisions based on the existing information. I must also remember this is an appeal hearing and not an actual trial by jury.

"Based on my interpretation of the current law, the defendants cannot leave the institution and live on their own accord. The provision is very exact and specifies that every person reaching the age of seventy must reside with a government facility if he or she cannot care for himself or herself independently. The rationale for the law is not our concern. A law is designed to govern each and every member of society, not just a select few.

"The defendant's attorney raises an interesting argument. It is true that the geriatric regulations are written in a singular format, but I do not interpret this as the ability for groups of citizens to depart from a facility, once accepted. Therefore, it is inappropriate to think that several senior citizens can violate an existing regulation. Living jointly is not acceptable within the confines of this particular law.

"I therefore judge the decision of this court in favor of the federal government. As with any appeal's verdict, no other recourse exists for the plaintiffs. All will spend the remainder of their lives at the government's facility. All of this can be changed, however, if the existing law is amended or repealed. If that occurs, then I will gladly reevaluate my decision."

No one uttered a sound. Everyone was in shock. The first sound was Rose Henderson softly sobbing as she attempted to comfort Inez. Harold Higgens tried to assure Stephen, Sarah, Ann, and Lyndel that he would do everything within his power to make their lives as normal as possible while at the facility.

Sylvester moved to a nearby window and gazed outside at the court's grass-filled yard. Feeling a hand gently touch his shoulder, he turned. Robin stood before him with tears flowing freely from the corner of each eye. He embraced his long-time friend. "I am very sorry…"

"There is nothing to be sorry about, you did your job well and for that I am proud. You have turned into an excellent attorney, but more importantly, a great human being."

"But the case…"

"We have wronged society and it is now up to you to correct it. I am no longer in a position to help."

"I will do my best. I give you my promise it will be changed."

"I believe you can accomplish it," the mentor said to his protégé.

"Now that I know where you are, would you mind if I visit you once in awhile?" Bradford asked.

Barlow smiled weakly, "Not at all."

Bailey joined Sylvester after Bradford left. "I am filled with regret; the decision was morally wrong."

"I know, but we tried. I want to thank you and your associates for all your time and assistance."

Ed gently hugged the elderly attorney.

The ride back to the facility was swift. No one spoke, and upon arriving, all went directly to their rooms. Solitude seemed their only solace from this personal defeat.

T W E N T Y - F O U R

B y mid-morning, Stephen and the others had congregated in the rotunda. Each sat quietly reading newspapers. "Have any of you seen Sylvester today?" Stephen inquired.

No one responded. A commotion in the hallway caused all to turn, but noting nothing unusual, they continued to read the papers. Many articles concerned the outcome of the trial. The reporters blasted the geriatric regulations and especially lambasted Judge Withers' decision. Every last reporter seemed committed to reshaping the government's philosophy and codes toward the country's geriatric population.

"Perhaps we did not lose in the long run," commented Ann.

"Let's see what Sylvester says after he sees the articles," said Stephen. "He'll know."

Head nurse Henderson wove through the living zombies until she reached the group. Noticing she was crying uncontrollably, Lyndel offered her a seat.

"What is wrong, Rose?"

She broke down completely at having to deliver the news: "It is Sylvester. He is dead."

The group flew back in their respective chairs in utter disbelief. "How?" questioned Inez.

"He killed himself sometime last night. The floor nurse discovered his body this morning. He cut his wrists...." She could not go on any further. Rose slouched forward and wept. "Why?" was all she could repeat. "Why did he do this to us..."

The group watched out the large window as a black station wagon arrived. From the bowels of the institution came a sheet-covered stretcher. It was lifted into the vehicle. Then everyone numbly gazed as it made its way slowly along the extended driveway.

No one said a word. They returned to their chairs and surveyed their now-permanent surroundings. There was little to say or do; instead each silently waited their turn.

Transplant

STANLEY L. ALPERT

O N E

Sandi Lee was a marvel for her age of eighty-four. Easily outlasting her three husbands, she continued to amaze even her five children. A graduate of New York University's Law School, she still maintained an active practice. As senior member of a medium-sized partnership, she had successfully guided her firm to its prestigious position.

Her age never seemed a detriment; in fact, she tended to use it to her best advantage. Utilizing the image of an elderly grandmother, Sandi maneuvered both judges and juries. Over the years, many decisions were won partially on her physical appearance. Opposing lawyers were gently lulled into a false security then skillfully manipulated by her accomplished articulation and abundant legal knowledge.

Her colleagues respected her apparently endless energy and the way she held the firm together. She was the driving force of Lee, Kramer, Gordon, and Weisberg, and every employee acknowledged this fact.

By 7:30 each weekday morning, the 4'11" woman arrived at work. The building's security guards would escort her to her office and then return to their posts. Because of her cheerful disposition, everyone considered her more a friend than an employer. She was always there when needed, and helped even entry-level employees. Sandi never asked anyone to perform a task she herself would not do. Despite her mild facade, she drove herself and her partners beyond anyone's expectations. Those unable to cope with her demands quickly left, but the ones remaining succeeded far above the norm, both financially and professionally.

Most of the firm's larger cases were handled by other senior partners; however, Sandi oversaw every major piece of litigation. She preferred to represent the less fortunate, and those cases that presented a legal challenge. Besides performing this full-time position, she was an active member of the American Bar Association, serving on several of its regional and national committees.

When not devoting her time to law, Sandi visited museums and enjoyed the cultural aspects of the city. Operas, symphonies, and ballets filled her busy schedule. As a sponsor and volunteer consultant to many of these artistic and cultural organizations, a great deal of her limited free time was devoted to their requests.

Despite these multiple obligations, she allowed herself ample time to enjoy her family. With most of her children and grandchildren living in the metropolitan area, spontaneous visits were commonplace, and gatherings were scheduled as frequently as possible.

Sandi attempted to accomplish as much as possible and to get the most out of life. She would frequently say, "Live for today." She fashioned her life on this creed.

T W O

The entire executive staff of Lee, Kramer, Gordon, and Weisberg was called to an emergency Saturday meeting by Warren Kramer. The principals sat around the colossal mahogany table that filled the conference room. Sandi addressed her partners.

"Warren and I are sorry to have called this meeting on such short notice, but due to extenuating circumstances, it simply could not wait. I am pleased to announce our firm has been selected to represent the Spartan Corporation in a forthcoming class-action suit."

Harold Gordon raised his hand. "When did we receive the news?"

"I received the telephone call around 5:00 yesterday afternoon. By then, all of you were gone," explained Sandi.

"Why did they select us?" asked Harold.

"I do not know exactly, nor did I question their criteria for making the choice. All I know is the job is ours," Sandi answered.

Warren interjected, "Sandi is being too modest, her reputation and vast experience in the field gave us the edge."

"What does the case involve?" continued Harold.

"I did not get all the details," said Sandi, "but I do think it may take us all the way to the Supreme Court. Ellen Bregman, their chief corporate counsel will be arriving within the hour. At that time, she will thoroughly brief us on the particulars."

"How are we going to handle the case within our organization?" inquired another attorney.

"Sandi will coordinate the entire operation. Since she was the key for obtaining the case, it seems only fitting that she control its destiny. Does anyone have any objections to the plan?" asked Warren.

Sandi acknowledged the nods of confidence, "I thank you for your faith in my abilities, but this venture will definitely require assistance from all of you. This must be a united effort. Now if you will all excuse me for a few minutes, I must attend to something. Warren will answer any other questions you might have."

Sandi left the room and rushed to the ladies' room; meanwhile, Harold and the other partners questioned Warren further. By the time Sandi returned to the room, Ellen Bregman was being formally introduced to the firm's senior partners.

Sandi assumed her seat at the head of the table and waited to be introduced. "Ms. Bregman, this is Sandi Lee, our founding partner."

Ellen walked to Sandi's side. "It is a pleasure to meet and work with you, Ms. Lee. I have looked forward to this for quite some time."

Sandi modestly replied, "I thank you, Ms. Bregman, and I hope our firm can assist you in this case. By the way, please call me Sandi."

"And call me Ellen." Sitting between Sandi and Harold, Bregman summarized the latest details of the litigation proceedings. With precision, she verbalized her company's position and anticipated results. "After all," she emphasized, "we have shareholders to answer to."

Throughout this period, Sandi listened intently and occasionally jotted down notes. Though the meeting was being taped, the elder attorney recorded significant bits of information. By the time Ellen was done, the entire group had questions. One by one, each partner resolved pertinent details and formulated their strategy. Sandi reserved any comments and listened intently to the discussion.

"What do you think, Sandi?" asked Warren.

"I am not sure. There have been several previous cases that may peripherally apply to this realm, but as far I know, it will be unique. I suggest our research department delve further. Personally, I cannot recall anything specific."

"What about Fielding v. Shane?" inquired Harold.

"That was different. The aspects of the case were different enough and besides, the Fielding Company lost the decision."

Ellen stated, "In the case of Hogan Corporation v. the State, Hogan won the decision."

"That is true, but the corporation was victorious because of a brilliant legal maneuver by their attorney, Charles White. The decision was later reversed by an upper court ruling. That judgment governed the policies of many corporations and is the aspect that must be attacked. It is the defense's weakest link," Sandi clarified.

The meeting continued, with only a short break for lunch. By the time darkness filled the skies, Harold called the conference to a halt. Ellen appeared content with her company's selection and particularly with Sandi's obvious expertise. Warren and Sandi remained after everyone else had departed.

"What do you think?" Warren asked.

"I believe we have a chance, but it is going to be difficult," Sandi answered.

"Do you have any objections to heading the case?"

"Not at all. I thought it was a foregone conclusion."

"Though I announced it before asking you, I just sensed you'd want the position. By the way, are you okay?"

"Certainly, why do you ask?"

"You left the meeting several times and I wondered..."

"Nonsense, I am not as young as I was and simply can't hold it as long, that's all." Warren grinned at her frankness. "Let's go enjoy the rest of the weekend and start on Monday."

"You go ahead. There is something I must do before leaving."

"Can I help?"

"Get out of here and get home to Margaret. I will be leaving shortly."

He obeyed her warm admonishment and exited. As soon as Sandi heard the outer office door close, she quickly examined the seat on which she had sat. Both the cushion and the back of her dress were wet. She cleaned the chair with a paper towel and headed home.

THREE

Early Monday morning, Sandi notified her office she would be late and requested that Warren start working with Ellen. She took a taxi to East 63rd Street and entered a brick building. After riding the elevator to the fifth floor, she found Suite 515.

"Good morning, Ms. Lee," said a voice from the receptionist's office. "The doctor will be with you shortly." Sandi sat on the plush sofa and waited. Ten minutes later, the voice came again, "Please go to the doctor's office; he will see you now."

"Thank you," said Sandi as she walked to the doctor's inner suite. Finding it empty, she waited.

Minutes later a middle-aged man walked into the room. "Well, Sandi, what is the problem?"

She explained her recent symptoms, including her frequent urgency to urinate. Dr. Thomas listened carefully. After taking her history, he thoroughly examined her. After drawing samples of blood and collecting a urine specimen, he concluded his examination with an electrocardiogram.

"Everything looks good, but I will call you when I get the results from the lab."

"What do you suspect?"

Knowing Sandi's age and professional status, Dr. Thomas carefully selected each word. "I will be checking to see if you have a bladder infection. Before I prescribe any medications, I must be sure of what I am dealing with."

"Do you have any thoughts?" Sandi pushed for an answer.

"I am not sure. Your symptoms are indicative of a great many things. Instead of guessing, I'll call you tomorrow when I receive the results."

Realizing Dr. Thomas could not satisfy her curiosity, Sandi returned to work. By the time she arrived at her office, Warren and Ellen were discussing the ramifications of the forthcoming litigation. Sandi quickly became engrossed in the conversation. The intensity of their conference acted as a buffer to divert her attention away from her physical condition.

Throughout the remainder of the day and into the next, the three lawyers worked steadily on the pending case. A gentle knocking at the door broke their concentration.

"Come in!" shouted Warren in a hostile tone. A young secretary cautiously peeked through the doorway. "Well, what do you want? I told everyone we were not to be disturbed for any reason!"

"I am sorry, but I have a personal call for Ms. Lee," she responded meekly.

All eyes turned to Sandi. She thought for a moment and then guessed the origin of the call. "I will be right back; please excuse me for a minute." As she exited the office, Sandi told the secretary, "I will be right there." She headed first to the ladies' room and then to her office.

"Hello, this is Sandi Lee."

"Please hold for the doctor. He will be right with you."

Nervously, Sandi waited. Finally a familiar voice spoke. "Hello, Sandi, are you there?" Dr. Thomas asked.

"Yes. What did you find?"

A man of few words, Dr. Thomas gave her the results. "The

tests show your white blood count is above normal and that your BUN is lower than what we consider normal."

"What does that mean?"

"It could be indicative of several things, but I'd like you to take another test."

"Another test? Why?"

"To eliminate certain possibilities and to help me correctly diagnose your situation."

"But I just had several tests."

"That is true, but they only gave us direction and eliminated possibilities. I must have more information at this point."

"Look, right now I am working on a very important case and can't get away. How long can we wait for the test?"

"Wait? You must be kidding! I want the test done within the next few days."

"Impossible."

"Sandi, you must find the time. I'm hoping it is simply a small bladder infection, but I don't want to be wrong. Besides, the tests can be done on an outpatient basis," Dr. Thomas urged.

"I'll try to rearrange my schedule."

"Good. Try calling Dr. Wegg; he is the most qualified to perform the test."

"I will call him later."

"Do you promise?"

Sandi did not answer his question, and returned the receiver to the cradle. She hesitated for a few minutes, then returned to the meeting.

F O U R

D r. Wegg was able to scheduled Sandi for an appointment to con-
form with her busy agenda. Though unpleasant, the cystomatrogram
was performed successfully.

After recovering, she met with the doctor in his office.
Mustering her strength, she asked, "What are the results?"

"It appears your bladder is functioning normally. The signs of
urinary control difficulty and bladder infection make me speculate
your problem is related to your kidneys."

"My kidneys?"

"Yes. All the evidence indicates some degree of renal failure."

"What is the prognosis?"

"It is impossible to tell at this time," Dr. Wegg explained.

Controlling her temper, Sandi asked, "You're the doctor, you
must have some idea of what's going on."

"Look, Ms. Lee, I am always up front with my patients. You are
no exception. I will call Dr. Thomas today with the results of the test
and it is then up to him to determine the next course of action."

Sandi returned to her office and summoned her private secretary. "Have Harvey get me all available information on renal failure.

Tell him I require it immediately and want every article placed on the computer's data service. Also have Jennifer call the medical library and obtain the latest literature on treatments."

After the door closed, Sandi began working on the Spartan project. The ringing of the phone aroused her from her research. "Yes, who is it?"

"There is a Dr. Thomas on the line."

"I will speak to him."

"Hello, Sandi," Dr. Thomas greeted her.

"I have been expecting your call."

"I thought you would be. I just got off the phone with Dr. Wegg. After going over the test results, I want you to schedule another appointment to see me on Monday."

"Monday I'm busy. I'll call at the end of next week."

"Sandi, you must get in here sooner," Dr. Thomas said bluntly, not wanting to alarm her.

"Look, with all due respect, I do not have a great deal of free time. Why don't we just save ourselves all the trouble. Send me a prescription for my problem and I'll send you a check for your time. That way, we'll both be happy," Sandi replied curtly.

"Sandi, I'm afraid it is not quite that simple. The appointment is essential and must be done as soon as possible," Dr. Thomas persisted.

"Why?"

"Let's just say it is a priority in your life."

"But my case..."

"It is secondary; we must address your kidneys' failure to fully function."

These somber words finally had an impact. Sandi scheduled an appointment and then called Warren. "Please come into my office." She presented her dilemma; without going into specifics, she explained seeing Drs. Thomas and Wegg and told briefly of their tentative diagnosis.

Warren listened and then asked, "But what about the case?"

"Tell Ellen I am doing research and will join the two of you shortly."

"She's been asking constantly to see you and I've had a hell of a time satisfying her demands."

"Do the best you can for now. Once I get to the bottom of this, I'll catch up on the facts."

He nodded and walked back to his office.

"The case?" Sandi cursed softly under her breath. "What about me?"

F I V E

Sandi focused on her job, and despite a great deal of discomfort and embarrassment, was able to camouflage her condition from Ellen and the rest of the law firm's staff. With their attack outlined, the senior legal department skillfully plotted their course. The elderly attorney's knowledge and abilities dominated each meeting. Ellen was especially impressed and continually seated herself at Sandi's side.

"Sandi, I am so glad you are handling this case for us. I wouldn't trust anyone else with the responsibility," Ellen said one morning.

"I thank you, but I am sure any of my partners could do the same job."

"I doubt it, but it is only academic. We have you and that is all that counts."

Every lunch hour, the two women ate together. A bond was developing between the two attorneys. Besides discussing the case and related legal topics, private aspects of their lives were revealed. Ellen had elected to forego a personal life and dedicated her life to her profession. Driven by an intrinsic quest for perfection, the young lawyer pushed herself beyond even her own expectations.

Working sixty hours a week was customary, but with her involvement in this litigation, Ellen labored seven full days a week.

"What do you do for excitement?" inquired Sandi one day.

"I enjoy my work," replied Ellen.

"What else do you do?"

Thinking for a moment, "Nothing, I simply love my work."

"Don't you date?"

"Periodically, but not too often."

"What are you doing Saturday night?"

"Working on this case. Why do you ask?" Ellen couldn't hide her curiosity.

"I happen to have an extra ticket to the John O'Regan concert. Would you like to go?"

"I don't think I can spare the time...."

"Nonsense, be my guest. We can discuss business before and after the concert."

"I'm not sure...."

"All right," quipped Sandi, "I won't bill your company for the time. It's on the house. Now what else could you ask for?"

Smiling, Ellen conceded, "I guess I could give up one evening."

They made arrangements and then continued to discuss the case.

SIX

At 6 p.m. sharp, Sandi's doorbell rang. "I'll be right there!" she shouted. When she opened the door, Sandi discovered her young friend. "Come on in, Ellen We have a few minutes to kill before leaving."

Ellen picked up an artifact from the coffee table. "What is this?"

"It is a good luck piece from Japan. I bought it during my last visit there."

"And this?"

"It is a small fragment of lava from Iceland. My late husband Charles was an amateur geologist. He collected all sorts of minerals and stones from around the world. Every time we'd go somewhere, we'd come back with lots of rocks."

"Did you see a lot of the world?"

"An awful lot of it. The only place I still want to see is Tibet."

"Tibet? Of all places, why Tibet?"

"I long to find the true answer of life. Perhaps I can locate it in one of those temples or from the Dalai Lama himself."

"When you find it, please tell me."

"Positively; we can share it." Looking at her watch, the elderly attorney gathered her coat. "We'd better get going."

Sandi insisted on driving. The symphony was an overwhelming success and John O'Regan's performance was outstanding. After the program, the two women went to Ellen's for a snack.

"Well?" inquired Sandi. "What did you think?"

"Never have I ever seen anything like it," responded Ellen.

"I was partial to the Rachmaninoff portion of the program, but all in all, John did a remarkable job tonight," Sandi commented.

"You refer to Mr. O'Regan as John. Do you know him personally?"

"I have met him on several occasions. The next time I attend another function, I'll bring you with me. He is a delightful person." Smirking slightly, Sandi added, "You know, you cannot discuss law with him…"

Ellen was feeling much more relaxed with Sandi as the elder woman shed her professional persona. They ate lightly. Anytime the topic drifted towards law or the Spartan case, Sandi instantly redirected it.

"Oh my goodness it's getting late, and I must be up early tomorrow," Ellen finally said.

"What's the hurry? The night is still young and tomorrow is Sunday. What is the urgency?" asked Sandi.

"I must examine several briefs," Ellen answered.

"Briefs? Forget it! Tomorrow, you're coming with me," insisted Sandi.

"But I can't, I must…"

"You must nothing. Everyone needs some time off. I will pick you up at 10 a.m. Be ready."

Not wanting to insult her newfound mentor, Ellen agreed. "I had a wonderful evening."

"Good, then you'll enjoy tomorrow even more."

"Where are we going? What do I wear?"

"Be ready at 10 a.m. Dress casually and wear walking shoes."

S E V E N

The two women were on the road the next morning. "I trust you slept well?" asked Sandi.

"Like a log, and I don't recall ever having such a good time. I still can't get over Mr. O'Regan's performance." Looking out the window at the passing scenery, Ellen asked, "Now are you going to tell me where we're going?"

"You will see soon enough. Just sit back and relax."

"Relax! That's a rare commodity. Perhaps after this case is settled, then I'll rest a little," Ellen said.

"After this one, they'll be another. Take it from an old warhorse; the battles are endless."

"I guess you're right."

"Of course I'm right. When is the last time you went on a vacation?"

"I really don't recall. It's been a long time."

"Perhaps you'd like to come to Tibet with me. We could both search for the true answer," suggested Sandi.

Laughing loudly, Ellen responded, "I don't think the company could get along without me for that much time." Instead of debating the issue, Sandi pointed to a roadside sign. "We're here."

"The Bronx Zoo? That's where we're going?"

"Certainly. This is a special day open only to its supporters. There will be no lines and very few people. By the way, when is the last time you were here?"

Thinking, Ellen responded, "God, it must be at least twenty years. I believe I came once with my parents."

"Well, you are in for quite a surprise." She guided the car into the main lot and led Ellen into the zoo. "Wait right here; I must go to the little girls' room a minute. While I am gone, study the brochure and let me know anything you would especially like to see."

For the rest of the day, the two explored. Giggling like two small children, they reveled in the many displays. Other than taking a periodic rest or allowing Sandi time for the ladies' room, the pair were in constant motion.

"Come on, slowpoke, we have one more thing to do before we leave," Sandi said mischievously.

"What else is left? I think we've seen everything!" exclaimed Ellen.

"Not quite, there is one more thing left." Taking her younger friend by the hand, Sandi pulled her along.

Reaching their destination, Ellen shrieked with delight. "Oh no you don't, I will not—"

"Where is your spirit? For an outgoing, dazzling attorney, you have certainly led a sheltered life!" teased Sandi.

Instead of arguing, Ellen permitted Sandi to whisk her to the front of the line. "Aren't you coming with me?" Ellen begged.

"Not today. You'll be safe. George is quite gentle. I've been on him many times before." Sandi watched as Ellen was seated on the back of a huge elephant. Once secure, George stood. "Have a good trip!" Sandi shouted as the animal started to walk. "Hopefully, I will see you soon. By the way, watch out for the tigers!" Ellen could not stop laughing.

"So how did you like the zoo?" asked Sandi on their way home.

"I still can't get over it. The whole thing was great."

"There is so much more to see. Unfortunately, creatures do not come to you."

"I suppose you are right. Someday, I want to go and…"

Sandi hoped her young friend had learned something that day. "Tomorrow I will be a little late. Harold will work with you until I arrive."

"Is everything okay?"

"Yes, why do you ask?"

"No reason. I was just concerned." Sandi dropped Ellen off at her apartment. "Thank you very much, I really had a wonderful weekend."

"Good, we'll do it again soon."

"I'd like that," Ellen said.

EIGHT

"Dr. Thomas will see you now." The nurse led Sandi through a maze of doorways until they reached the doctor's consultation room. "Please have a seat, the doctor will be right with you."

A few minutes later the door opened and Dr. Thomas entered the room with chart in hand. He leafed through the various papers that filled the file. Finally he asked, "So tell me, Sandi, how are you feeling today?"

Trying to contain herself, she responded. "Fine, now what is this great urgency?"

Looking downward at the open chart, "There is a problem with your last test."

"Doctor, I do not have time for this nonsense. Just tell me plain and simple, what is wrong?"

"Your kidneys are not functioning properly."

"I have taken it upon myself to do some reading on the subject. What will be your course of action?" Sandi said.

The physician responded, "Only two things will work in your case, and those are dialysis or a transplant."

"From what I have read thus far, you are correct. Where do I get a kidney and how long will the recovery period be? I must get back to the case I'm working on."

"Sandi, I don't think you fully comprehend the seriousness of the problem," Dr. Thomas said gently.

"Look, I am a lawyer, not a doctor. Healing the sick is your job, not mine. Just tell me what to do and I'll do it. I don't have time for any of this."

"Well, getting a kidney is difficult. Once it is obtained and confirmed to be compatible, the risk of surgery must be considered. At eighty-four, you are not considered a good surgical candidate."

"Look, I don't care about statistics. Just get this thing going and tell me what I need to do in the meantime."

Dr. Thomas prescribed several medications and then called the kidney division of Albert Einstein College of Medicine. "I want you to make arrangements to see a Dr. Santiago. He will take over your case."

"Why?"

"He is the world's leading authority on transplants and heads the department. If anyone can help, it will be him."

Sandi took the number and left for her office. Looking at the name, she muttered, "Kidneys! Who has time for this?"

NINE

Everyone looked up as Sandi entered the room. Ellen smiled then continued her work with Harold. Within minutes, Sandi was caught up in the momentum of the business at hand. Throughout the remainder of the day, they labored. Finally, at 4 p.m. they called it a day.

Returning to her office, Sandi picked up the phone, "Sally, get me David Goldman."

"Mr. Goldman's office."

"Dave Goldman, please."

"May I ask who is speaking?"

"This is Sandi Lee. Tell him it is important."

Seconds later, the head of the firm's malpractice division was on the line. "Ms. Lee, this is David Goldman. How can I help you?"

"I want you to find out as much as you can about a Dr. Santiago at the Albert Einstein College of Medicine. He is a kidney specialist."

"Do you have a first name?"

"No, but I'm sure you can get the information."

"I will try."

"I want it on my desk by tomorrow and this matter is to remain strictly confidential. Do you understand?"

"Yes, Ms. Lee. You can trust me."

Without hanging up, she made another call. "Hello, Jessie, this is Sandi."

"Sandi, it is a pleasure to hear from you. It's been such a long time..."

"I agree. Look, darling, I need a big favor."

"Anything. After all the things you have done for me, ask away."

"I want you to find out who the big shots are at Albert Einstein College of Medicine. I want a list of the board, fund raisers, and anyone else of any consequence at the place."

"I know several of them personally, but I will get the rest as soon as possible."

"Thanks, and I hope to see you soon."

"Me too. By the way, is everything okay?"

"Yes, I just need the information for a big case," Sandi lied. She went to the rest room then returned to her office. A short time later, Ellen entered. "Sandi, are you okay?"

"Yes. Why do you ask?"

"Just curious. That's all."

Attempting to change the subject, Sandi said, "By the way, I have been invited to a special showing at a small village gallery. Are you free this weekend?"

"I have too much to do."

"Work?"

"Why, yes, of course."

"Good, then it's settled. We're going," stated Sandi emphatically.

"I really don't think so. I simply do not have the free time."

"We will only stay a short time, I promise!" Relenting, Ellen agreed. "Good. It's better than sitting around and working all the time. Besides, perhaps we can find you a poor, starving, potentially successful artist."

"Get that thought out of your mind."

"I was only kidding. See you tomorrow and I'm sorry about

missing part of the meeting."

"It's okay. Actually, Harold is quite a competent attorney."

"I know. I handpicked him for the case."

T E N

Sandi examined the information David Goldman had accumulated. To herself she muttered, "Dr. Santiago, let's just see what you are all about." Besides graduating first in his class at medical school, his professional credentials were impeccable. Nothing indicated any flaws in his background. Besides being the recipient of numerous awards and accolades, his list of published articles and books was impressive and lengthy.

Closing the file, Sandi sat back in her oversized chair and thought, *Well, Dr. Santiago, it seems we are going to be doing some business together.* Picking up the phone, she dialed the doctor's office and scheduled an appointment.

For the next few days, Sandi, Ellen, and Harold worked diligently on the Spartan case. Other than short breaks, they toiled from dawn to dusk. By Friday all were exhausted.

"Ellen, I'll pick you up tomorrow at 1 p.m."

"Why don't we forget it; we're both tired," Ellen suggested.

"Rubbish, it will do us good to get out."

"Then let me drive this time; you drove last."

"Fine, I'll be ready at 1 p.m."

At precisely 1 p.m., Ellen pulled up to Sandi's home. She waited several minutes at the door after knocking. Finally she rang the bell. When no one answered, she turned the handle and to Ellen's surprise, the door moved inward. Sticking just her head inside, she looked around and then yelled, "Sandi, are you here?" Hearing nothing, she walked into the entry and waited.

Alarmed by the prolonged silence, Ellen moved through the living room and into the kitchen. Again she shouted, but heard nothing. Climbing the stairs, she wandered around the second floor until she reached the master bedroom.

There she discovered Sandi lying in her nightgown in the middle of the bed. "Sandi! Are you okay?" Ellen asked anxiously.

The elderly woman stirred. Ellen approached the bed and gently touched her friend. "Sandi, wake up. Are you okay?"

Sandi pulled herself upright and stared at Ellen. "What happened? What are you doing here?"

"It's past 1 p.m. when we agreed I'd pick you up. When I found your front door open, I decided to see where you were."

"I guess I overslept. I'm sorry, please forgive me..." In an attempt to stand, Sandi fell back onto the bed.

"What is wrong? Are you ill?"

"No, I'm just a little disoriented. Give me a minute and I'll get dressed." Ellen watched as Sandi collected her senses.

Finally, in a respectful but stern tone, Ellen said, "Sandi, I'm worried about you. Tell me who to call."

"No one. I'll be just fine. I guess the case has gotten to me; I'm not as young as I used to be."

"Let me call your children."

"My children and I are exactly the same. Like acorns from a tree. They will not be of any assistance. Please do not worry. I am sure everything will be just fine."

After some time for reorientation, Sandi was finally able to dress herself. Instead of going to the gallery, the two women chose to remain where they were and had an enjoyable afternoon together.

ELEVEN

Ellen called Sandi several times on Sunday to check on her status. The elderly woman spent the day either in bed or on the sofa. Again the younger woman tried to get permission to call Sandi's children, but relented under unfaltering opposition.

"Are you eating?" asked Ellen.

"Stop worrying about me. I'll see you in the office tomorrow and be prepared to work," Sandi replied reassuringly.

Sandi arrived at her usual time to scrutinize several abstracts. She analyzed their potential for the ensuing case. Harold soon entered the room and, after a brief greeting, started assisting his partner. Others filtered in and within no time everybody was present except for Ellen. Hours later, she arrived and sat at Sandi's side. Without explaining her tardiness, Ellen opened her attaché case, withdrew several papers, and entered the discussion.

During the lunch break, Ellen joined Sandi in her office. "How are you feeling?"

"Everything is good. I told you not to worry. By the way, I was concerned over your lateness."

"I had a few things to do before coming," answered Ellen

vaguely.

Without questioning one another further, the two walked back to the main conference area. Sandi asked, "I was wondering if you'd like to go to the gallery this coming weekend?"

"Yes, as long as you promise to be in good health."

"I'll try," she laughed. "By the way, would you meet with Harold and Warren tomorrow? I'm taking part of the day off."

"Off? But the case?"

"I'll be back by 2 p.m. Both Harold and Warren know what must be done."

"It's just that I prefer to work with you," Ellen said.

"I understand, but this appointment is pressing. I will return as quickly as possible, I promise."

T W E L V E

"Ms. Lee," said a middle-aged, handsome dark man.

"Yes, and you must be Dr. Santiago."

They sat opposite each other as the physician addressed the small woman.

"It appears from everything here that your kidneys have a problem. I would like to examine you to help formulate a better idea of your situation."

He spent almost an hour performing a physical examination. While she dressed, he reviewed her medical record.

"Well, doctor, what do you think?"

"I'm afraid my initial suspicions were correct. I believe you are in renal failure."

"Are you positive?" Sandi asked as she slumped back in her seat.

"I'm nearly one-hundred percent sure. Everything else has been ruled out. I wish, of course, I was wrong." Sandi remained silent while the experienced physician continued, "You can go for another opinion should you desire."

"I don't think that is necessary. I've already done my homework about my condition and your credentials." Struggling to maintain her composure, she asked, "What do I do next?"

"I recommend dialysis. Hopefully, it will do the trick."

"What if it doesn't?"

"We can cross that bridge when we come to it."

" Is a transplant the next bridge?"

"Yes, but let's remain optimistic. Many of my patients respond nicely to dialysis. I feel your chances are quite good. Assuming, of course, we begin immediately."

"Immediately? I can't. I'm involved in a critical case...."

"I'm afraid the case will have to either wait or work itself around your therapy schedule." Deliberately not waiting for an answer, Dr. Santiago scheduled an appointment for his patient. After hanging up the phone he said, "Well, Sandi, we're in luck. They can fit you in tomorrow at 10 a.m."

"Tomorrow! I can't just drop everything..." she said defiantly.

"When it comes to your health, you have no choice," the doctor stated.

"Can I wait a little longer?"

"No," he responded in an authoritarian manner. Then he added, "Sandi, there can be no delay. I am truly sorry."

After leaving his office, Sandi walked slowly to her car. Once inside, she looked at her reflection in the mirror. Suddenly, she wept uncontrollably.

THIRTEEN

Everyone sat around the conference table while Sandi listened to discussions and debates throughout the afternoon. Their work seemed to be systematically organizing itself. Satisfied with the results, she added little to the dialogue. By 5 p.m. everyone adjourned, except for the firm's senior partners and Ellen.

"Well, what do you think?" inquired Warren of Ellen.

"I am very pleased so far. I have already reported to my company and they are extremely satisfied with our progress," Ellen said.

Harold summarized several more points and then requested that the meeting be adjourned. Everyone agreed—until Sandi stood and asked for everyone's attention. "I'm sorry to hold everyone up, but something has come up that must be discussed immediately. I will not be present for portions of our meetings over the next few weeks. Something important has come up and I am required to be elsewhere. During those times, however, I will be working on the case."

Harold asked, "Will you be handling the case in court?"

"I am not sure. Let's take one step at a time. If everything goes as planned, I foresee no problems."

Ellen sat silently as the partners continued their interrogation.

255

"Is anything wrong?" asked Harold.

"I am having a small physical problem and must undergo a course of treatments. Hopefully they will work quickly."

"Is it serious?"

"Anything can be serious, but I do expect to be your senior partner for a while longer," Sandi smiled reassuringly.

Out of respect, no one said another word as they left the room. Warren and Sandi remained. "What else have your doctors learned since we talked about this last?" Sandi's long-time partner and friend asked.

"My kidneys are not functioning. I must undergo renal dialysis."

"Can't you stall for time? This case is so damn important for our group."

"Warren, I fully comprehend the possible repercussions upon our firm, but you must understand my dilemma."

"I do and you have my full support. Have you, by the way, gotten another opinion?"

"Everything has been checked out and confirmed. I start tomorrow at 10 a.m."

"So soon?"

"Yes. I will return by 2 p.m."

Sighing Warren mused, "I guess you have no choice. I only hope Spartan does not look for another firm."

Sandi watched as her partner left the room. She gazed at the huge empty conference room and at the pictures on the wall. Having given the majority of her life's energy to the firm, a sense of disillusionment leaked into her thinking. Standing, she gathered her papers and returned home for the evening.

FOURTEEN

A ringing of her doorbell caused Sandi to jump. Walking to the door, she asked, "Who is it?"

"Ellen. May I come in?"

Opening the door slightly, Sandi peeked outside and observed her friend standing at her entrance. "What? Yes, come in."

Once inside, the young attorney sat. "Sandi, I am very worried about you."

"Worried? What are you worried about?"

"I know something is wrong. Please tell me what it is."

Sitting on her sofa, Sandi looked at her newly acquired friend, "I have renal failure."

"Renal failure! What can we do?"

"I begin dialysis treatments tomorrow at 10 a.m. Hopefully that will solve the problem."

"Have you sought another opinion?"

"I am satisfied where I am."

"I will go with you."

"No, you are needed at the meetings. I will be fine."

"Have you told your children?"

"Not all the details, but they are aware of the situation. If I really need them, they will come. By the way, my daughter Carol told me you called her. That was very considerate of you."

"You aren't mad at me for contacting her?" Ellen asked guiltily.

"Not at all, just flattered."

"What if the dialysis doesn't work?"

"There is only one choice left: a kidney transplant."

"Oh!"

"Let's not think along those lines." Trying to change the subject Sandi added, "Have you eaten yet?"

"No, I was too upset."

"Good, let's go out and celebrate. I know of a nice quiet restaurant around the corner. We can discuss business if you'd like."

"What are we celebrating?"

"Life!"

F I F T E E N

Sandi arrived at exactly 10 a.m. and met Dr. Santiago. After reviewing the procedure and familiarizing her with the facility and staff, he prepared her for the session. Once in process, Sandi relaxed and studied the elaborate machinery as it cleansed her body of its insidious wastes. "It's amazing," she marveled.

"Not really, just science and medicine. How do you feel?" asked her doctor.

"Not really any different." Dr. Santiago took notes then excused himself. "I will see you before you leave." Sandi looked around a while longer and then read several briefs pertaining to her upcoming case.

Three hours later, she was disconnected from the machinery. "Is that all there is?" she asked hopefully.

"Yes. We have scheduled you for three times a week at 10 a.m."

"Can't we make it another time? I do have my work..."

"This is the only available time. In fact, I had to fight to get it for you; other doctors also need it for their patients. Since I head the department and because of the urgency of your physical status, I was able to move you ahead on the waiting list."

By the time Sandi arrived at her office, the meeting was in full swing. She took a more passive role and spoke only when specifically addressed. Harold and Ellen had the entire situation well in hand.

During a brief break, Ellen questioned her about the treatment. "Stop worrying so much!" Sandi interrupted her. "Let's discuss this case. After all, that's what your company is paying us for."

The young attorney outlined the day's progress. "What do you think?"

"Excellent job. You are to be commended."

"Do we really stand a good chance?" queried Ellen.

"Honestly, I'm not sure, but I do think we have at least a fifty percent chance of winning. The mood of the court may be in our favor. I just sense it. Years ago, we wouldn't have had a chance, but things are different today. Yes, I believe we can do it."

"By the way, what are you doing for supper tonight?" asked Ellen.

"Nothing, why do you ask?" replied Sandi.

"I'd like to invite you out if you're up to it."

"Fine, but I must make it an early evening. I am tired from the dialysis."

After a delightful dinner, Sandi went home and spoke to her daughter Carol. Knowing her eldest daughter would convey her messages to the other children, she then relaxed on the sofa and listened to her favorite classical piece. Soon she fell into a peaceful sleep.

SIXTEEN

Weeks passed and Sandi continued her treatments at the Albert Einstein College of Medicine Kidney Center. Her relationship with Dr. Santiago became one of mutual admiration. He went out of his way to say hello every time she arrived for her therapy and he personally directed the entire process.

Despite the therapy, the elderly attorney's body steadily worsened. Dr. Santiago tried every method within the field of nephrology and dialysis, but nothing seemed to be working. Responding to her body's failures, Sandi's functional level decreased. Simple tasks became difficult or impossible to perform.

This decline was also altering the lives of Sandi's colleagues; her legal firm installed a special telephone communication device at her home and at the dialysis center so she was "present" for all meetings. Her expertise and input were still necessary for the success of the case. Ellen was always at her side and elected to work exclusively in this way. Since the preparations were being accomplished, no one had any objections to the unusual system. Often Sandi would merely listen. Saving her limited energies, she usually spoke only when spoken to.

Sandi's daughter Carol, having recently gone through a divorce, decided to spend some time with her mother. She, along with Ellen, cared for the elderly attorney's needs. Despite the decline in her condition, Sandi's spirits remained high and her enthusiasm never seemed to falter.

Taking a break during a particularly intense meeting, Sandi turned off the communication device at the center. She smiled at her friend, "Tell me, Ellen, what do you think of Dr. Santiago?"

"I think he is a very thorough and good physician."

"Is that all?"

"I'm not sure I understand the gist of your question."

"Let me rephrase it another way. Did you know he is single?"

"It never crossed my mind one way or the other. What are you trying to do anyway?"

Smiling knowingly, Sandi replied, "Oh, nothing. Nothing at all."

"Don't you dare!" Ellen chuckled. "He's very nice and all that, but I don't have time for anything like that. I'm much too busy with the case and you. Promise me you won't say or do anything."

Sandi refused to promise, but instead turned on the telephone device and asked for Warren. After first communicating with him concerning the forthcoming case, everyone else joined in the discussion. With a court date set, everyone was working feverishly to solidify their defense.

SEVENTEEN

"Sandi, I'd like to speak with you for a moment, if you can spare the time," Dr. Santiago asked.

"Certainly."

"I mean alone," he continued, indicating Ellen's presence. Sandi left Ellen and accompanied her physician into an office. "I'd like to discuss several things that are on my mind. I know your case is only two weeks away, but I feel this is equally important."

"What is it?"

"It's your progress. I'm not satisfied with the way you are responding to the dialysis. For some reason you're not getting any better under our present regimen and are, in fact, worsening."

"I see," said Sandi, not surprised.

"I feel we should consider a transplant at this point."

"Fine. Do what you have to do and I will consent. I fully trust your judgment."

"I'm afraid it is not quite so simple. But before I go into all the details, let me run a few other tests to determine if you are even a suitable candidate."

Sandi replied, "Should I study for them?"

Caught off guard, the serious doctor tried to answer: "I do not think that you could...." Realizing his own inappropriate response, Santiago's shoulders relaxed and he smiled, "Sandi, you are indeed a remarkable woman."

"Do you mean I'm remarkable as a woman, or for my age?"

"For your age, of course."

"I guess I should take that as a compliment, but I never considered my age to be a factor. I will continue to live until I die," Sandi stated.

"I will let you know the results of the tests within a few days," Dr. Santiago promised.

"Fine. By the way, do you have a steady girlfriend?"

Taken aback by the question, Santiago turned defensive, "Why do you ask?"

"I was just curious."

"Curious?"

"Yes, I'm just interested about the man in my life," quipped Sandi.

"Honestly, I've always been too busy to date or even socialize. My work is my life, and therefore I have little time to see anyone. Besides, no one could understand this dedication."

"What are you smiling at?" inquired Ellen as they approached her in the waiting room.

"I didn't realize I was smiling. No reason at all, I was just thinking about something humorous," answered Sandi.

EIGHTEEN

Despite her compromised health, Sandi continued to contribute greatly to the case as they labored to complete the final preparations. Harold and Ellen would perform most of the courtroom work, with assistance from Sandi whenever possible; Warren and the others would supply the necessary backup when necessary.

Two days before the actual trial was to begin, the chief officers from Spartan came to the offices of Lee, Kramer, Gordon, and Weisberg. Sandi sat at Ellen's side as both she and Harold outlined their plan. After hours of discussion and questioning, everyone present seemed satisfied.

The chairman of the board of Spartan turned to his corporate counselor. "Your selection was the right one for our company. They are exactly what you said they would be and more." Looking at Sandi, he continued, "I want to thank you personally for all your help and wish you well in the future. Hopefully we will both win our battles."

"I thank you and only want to add that your company is blessed with a gifted attorney. The reasons for our achievements thus far have been her motivation, skill, and knowledge. Indeed, it has been our privilege to work with your company and especially with such a capable corporate lawyer." Turning to Ellen, Sandi added, "Should you ever desire to join a private firm, you are more than welcome here."

"I'm afraid she's not going anywhere. After this is over, Ellen is being promoted to the position of vice president," announced the chairman." Everyone stood and applauded.

"I thank you all for the honors, but I'd rather celebrate after our courtroom victory," was Ellen's modest response. The group broke into smaller fractions and finally dispersed. Ellen drove Sandi home.

"How about coming in for awhile?" asked Sandi.

"I don't think so tonight. I am very tired. You visit with Carol," replied Ellen.

"By the way, congratulations on your promotion," Sandi said.

"We'll see. Right now I want to get through the case."

NINETEEN

"Hello, Sandi?"

"Yes."

"This is Dr. Santiago. I'm sorry to bother you so late, but I just got the results back from the lab."

"Oh," replied Sandi realizing she had temporarily forgotten about the tests. "Yes, what were they?"

"All very good. You have an excellent match of antigens, no negative antibodies, and your blood type is A positive."

"Is that good?"

"Yes. All three are conducive to transplanting. I will see you tomorrow during your treatment to discuss our next step."

Sandi looked at herself in the mirror and for the first time saw a pathetic aged body. From the disease, her physique was wasting away and there was nothing she could do to prevent it. "Hopefully, the transplant will work," she uttered as she slid into bed. "I don't want to die."

TWENTY

D r. Santiago sat down next to Sandi. "You don't mind if Ellen stays?" asked Sandi.

"Not at all." Getting right to the point, he said, "Transplanting has been around for quite awhile and is surgically quite simple at this point. Of course, there is always an element of risk involved in any surgical intervention, but this procedure is very systematized. Failures usually come from rejection and not the surgical procedure itself. The real problem is obtaining a kidney. With the current state of affairs, few kidneys are available."

"Why is that?" inquired Ellen.

"Very few people donate their organs and with the increased number of kidney patients, only a select few are even considered."

"Who makes the choice?" asked Sandi.

"Here at Albert Einstein, we have a committee that determines who shall receive a kidney or other organ for transplanting."

"Who serves on the committee?" Sandi asked.

"Sandi, I can only tell you I am one of the members. The rest must remain anonymous."

"When will they decide on me?"

"I will bring your name up as a possible candidate next week and you should hear within a month."

At this point, Ellen interrupted. "Why so long? If Sandi needs a kidney, I'll give her one of mine."

"As with any major decision, every possible avenue must first be explored. Should anyone specific desire to donate a kidney, then we will perform the appropriate test to determine its compatibility. If a volunteer's organ checks out, then there would be no need to wait for the committee's decision; we could operate immediately."

"What are my chances?" asked Sandi.

"If selected by the committee, I'd say your chances of living will be quite good."

After her session, Sandi had Ellen drive her to the office. "Ellen, you go home and prepare yourself for the trial. There is something I must do and then I'll have Carol pick me up here."

"I'll wait," replied Ellen.

"No, I insist. I will see you in court tomorrow."

After Ellen left, Sandi picked up the phone. After obtaining the information from Jessie, the elderly attorney asked her senior partners to meet with her. Though very busy and anxious over tomorrow's case, all attended. "I need a very big favor from each of you. I would like to have the following persons contacted immediately and passively persuaded to influence the transplant committee in my favor. Use whatever means or resources available, but it must be done effectively. I would also like our firm to donate a large sum of money to the Albert Einstein Kidney Center and make sure my name is known as the prime force behind the action. Can anyone else think of anything?"

Several other suggestions were given and delegated. Once assured everyone knew their tasks, Sandi called her daughter and went home to prepare for her day in court.

TWENTY-ONE

The next few days went smoothly both in the courtroom and at the hospital. Though all of Sandi's potential donors were rejected, her attitude was still very optimistic. She was formally notified that her name had been added to the transplant committee's existing list and, through the grapevine, she was assured of being given preferential consideration. Because of her firm's incredibly generous donation to the Kidney Center, Sandi sensed her acceptance was a mere formality.

On the legal front, Ellen was skillfully manipulating the hearings in her favor. The young attorney quickly won over the jury with her innocence and sweetness. Her opposition's case was crude and unpolished; the pendulum swung easily toward the Spartan team. Sandi's captivating presence and articulate mannerisms capped the verdict. Weakened by her disease process, she capitalized on the jury's sentiments. Her summation was a thing of beauty as she selected every word with precision. She efficiently dissected her opponent's position and argument, and proved beyond any reasonable doubt that Spartan was in the right. It took only a few hours for the verdict to be finalized. All ears listened as the decision was read. "We, the jury, find Spartan Corporation not guilty..."

Sandi slouched in her seat as the others hugged and cheered one another. Ellen tenderly grasped her mentor's hand. "Well, it looks as if you've won another one."

"I did not win anything. It was a combined effort by all of us. I am just glad to be part of the winning team."

The officers of Spartan were ecstatic over the decision and rewarded Lee, Kramer, Gordon, and Weisberg with a long-term consulting contract. Everyone went out to celebrate. "Sandi, why don't you join us?" asked Ellen.

"I'm not up to it. You go and have a good time. I think I better go home and rest."

Ellen kissed her friend on the cheek. "I'll call you in the morning."

TWENTY-TWO

Ellen became nervous when neither Sandi nor Carol answered her calls. Finally, out of desperation, she called another one of Sandi's children. Pauline told her of her mother's unforeseen setback and of her emergency hospitalization during the night. "I guess the work and trial were simply too much for her," she surmised.

"Why did she do it, if it was too much for her? Her firm certainly didn't need the business that badly. Why?" asked Ellen.

"Perhaps you should ask her," was Pauline's only reply.

"I will."

She hung up the phone and hurried to the hospital. Carol met her in the waiting room. "How is she?"

"Not good. Dr. Santiago will be arriving soon."

"Can I see her?"

"Yes, she's in Room 10."

Ellen entered the room and was shocked at the sight. Sandi was attached to an IV and several other monitors. The young woman sat down at Sandi's side. "Why?" she asked. "Why did you push yourself? It was only a case."

"I did it for you," came the sobering reply.

"For me?"

"Yes. I knew it meant a great deal to you and to your future."
Their conversation was interrupted by the entrance of Dr. Santiago.

"Please help her," Ellen cried as she grabbed his arm. "Please,
I beg you."

"Let me examine her and I will see you and Carol in the lobby,"
Dr. Santiago replied gently.

Ellen pleaded, "Please help her."

"I'll see what I can do, now go to the lobby. I'll be there as soon
as I see what is happening."

Ellen kissed her friend on the forehead. "I'll be right back."

"I'll be here," Sandi smiled weakly. "It seems I won't be going
anywhere for a while."

Ellen returned to the lobby and waited with Carol. Some time
later, Dr. Santiago met with them. "Things are not going too well.
She is much worse than expected."

"What about a transplant?"

"I have called an emergency meeting of the committee. We will
be meeting tonight."

"Will they make a definite decision tonight?"

"I will demand it. If she does not have the surgery soon, I'm
afraid her chances are very poor."

Ellen spontaneously took his hand, "Please help us."

"I will do everything within my power," said Dr. Santiago reassuringly.

Both women returned to keep Sandi company. All they could
do was wait.

TWENTY-THREE

"Ellen?"

"Yes?"

"This is Carol."

"What's happening there at the hospital?"

"I just heard from Dr. Santiago. The committee met last night and rejected my mother for the transplant."

"Why? How could they?"

"It seems only one kidney is available and there are several people in desperate need of it."

"Why not her?"

"According to Dr. Santiago, the others are all much younger."

"One is a teenager who must have immediate surgery to live."

"So does your mother! Since when is age the criteria? That's discrimination!"

"I agree, but the committee has made its decision and the young person is already in surgery."

"What about your mother? What is going to happen?"

"Unless there is a miracle, she is going to—" Carol couldn't finish her sentence.

Ellen slowly placed the telephone down beside her bed. Anger, hatred, sadness, sorrow, and disgust all stampeded through her thoughts. Dressing quickly, she left for the hospital.

Sandi was alone in the room when she entered. Ellen pulled a chair to her side and took her hand. Sandi said flatly, "I already know. Carol has told me of the committee's decision."

"How could they? How could he do this to you?" responded Ellen.

"It was not Dr. Santiago's fault. He was the sole member who voted in my behalf."

Crying, Ellen lost control, "Oh Sandi, what are we going to do?"

"There is nothing we can do. We must accept their decision and prepare for the inevitable."

"But—"

"We all must die sometime; I am not afraid of death. Yes, I would have preferred to live longer, but sometimes there is simply no choice. Each of us must face this fate; I am lucky for the life I have lived." Stroking Ellen's hair, Sandi continued, "To waste a life is not to have lived at all. Examine your priorities and values, and then determine your course. Don't ever bargain, sacrifice, or settle for less when charting your destiny. If you do, then you're compromising whatever valuable time you have remaining. Each of us is here on a brief visit. This is not a stage nor is life a rehearsal; savor each precious moment."

Ellen sobbed and dropped her head to her friend's chest. "Don't cry for me, my little friend," Sandi said trying to soothe her. "I will never forget you and someday, perhaps, we will meet again." Kissing Ellen on the cheek, Sandi said, "Now go and get Carol, she should be here by now."

Turning at the doorway, Ellen spoke, "I love you."

"And I love you," Sandi replied.

Sandi's children were all waiting in the lobby when Ellen arrived. They walked dejectedly to their mother's room. Ellen waited respectfully outside. Finally, it was Carol who returned. One look and Ellen knew exactly what had transpired.

"She's dead, isn't she?"

"Yes," sobbed Carol. "She died a few minutes after we arrived. She just closed her eyes and went to sleep." The two women held one another for the longest time. Neither could speak as sorrow invaded their bodies. Reaching into her pocket, Carol extracted a small white envelope and handed it to Ellen. "My mother's final words were to give this to you. She said you would know what to do with it."

With a trembling hand, the young attorney took the envelope and looked inside. She withdrew the piece of paper and studied it closely. Smiling through tears, she placed it in her pocket. She kissed Carol once more then walked dejectedly to her car.

Sitting in the parking lot, she withdrew the ticket once more. *Yes, Sandi, I know what to do.* She placed the round-trip ticket to Tibet safely within her purse and returned to her apartment. The next day she resigned from her position at Spartan and prepared to depart as soon as Sandi's funeral was over.

Other books by Stanley L. Alpert

GERTRUDE AND THE PRINTED PAGE

MOHOP MOGANDE

A ROOMFUL OF PARADOX

Available from

Alpert's Bookery, Inc.
POB 215
Nanuet, NY 10954